THE USBORNE PICTURE DICTIONARY IN GERMAN

Felicity Brooks and Fiona Chandler
Designer and modelmaker: Jo Litchfield

German language consultant: Barbara Bethäußer-Conte

Design and additional illustrations by
Mike Olley and Brian Voakes

Photography by Howard Allman

Contents

How to say the words

You can hear all the German words in this book, read by a German person,
on the Usborne Quicklinks Website at **www.usborne-quicklinks.com**
All you need is an Internet connection and a computer that can
play sounds. Find out more on page 112.

Using your dictionary

You can use this dictionary to find out how to say things in German. Each page has 12 main words in English, with the same words in German (the translations).

The English words are in the order of the alphabet: words beginning with A are first in the book. There are also pictures to show what words mean.

This letter in a blue square shows the first letter of the English words on that page.

This word shows the first English word on the page.

This word shows the last English word on the page.

All the English words are shown in blue. The German translations are shown in black.

Don't forget that in a dictionary you read down the page in columns. In most other books you read across.

Short sentences or phrases, in English and in German, show you how the word can be used.

If you forget the order of the letters in the alphabet, look at the bottom of any page.

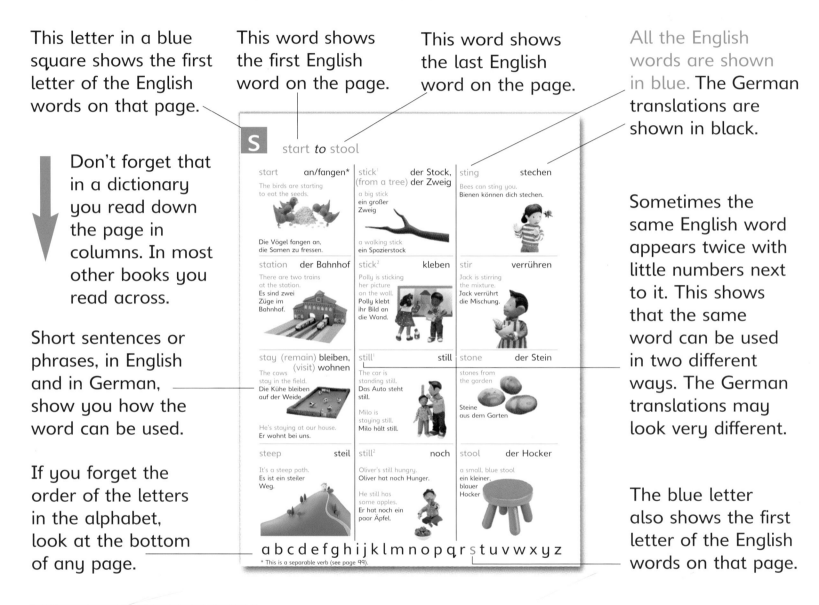

S

start to stool

start   an/fangen*
The birds are starting to eat the seeds.
Die Vögel fangen an, die Samen zu fressen.

station   der Bahnhof
There are two trains at the station.
Es sind zwei Züge im Bahnhof.

stay (remain) bleiben, (visit) wohnen
The cows stay in the field.
Die Kühe bleiben auf der Weide.
He's staying at our house.
Er wohnt bei uns.

steep   steil
It's a steep path.
Es ist ein steiler Weg.

stick[1]   der Stock, (from a tree) der Zweig
a big stick
ein großer Zweig
a walking stick
ein Spazierstock

stick[2]   kleben
Polly is sticking her picture on the wall.
Polly klebt ihr Bild an die Wand.

still[1]   still
The car is standing still.
Das Auto steht still.
Milo is staying still.
Milo hält still.

still[2]   noch
Oliver's still hungry.
Oliver hat noch Hunger.
He still has some apples.
Er hat noch ein paar Äpfel.

sting   stechen
Bees can sting you.
Bienen können dich stechen.

stir   verrühren
Jack is stirring the mixture.
Jack verrührt die Mischung.

stone   der Stein
stones from the garden
Steine aus dem Garten

stool   der Hocker
a small, blue stool
ein kleiner, blauer Hocker

a b c d e f g h i j k l m n o p q r s t u v w x y z
* This is a separable verb (see page 99).

Sometimes the same English word appears twice with little numbers next to it. This shows that the same word can be used in two different ways. The German translations may look very different.

The blue letter also shows the first letter of the English words on that page.

How to find a word

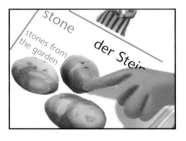

1 Think of the letter the word starts with. "Stone" starts with an "s," for example.

2 Look through the dictionary until you have found the "s" pages.

3 Think of the next letter of the word. Look for words that begin with "st."

4 Now look down all the "st" words until you find your word.

2

Der, die or das?

In German, all nouns, or "naming" words such as "boy," "woman" and "house," are either masculine, feminine or neuter. The German word for "the" is *der* for masculine nouns, *die* for feminine nouns and *das* for neuter nouns.

You can sometimes guess whether a noun is masculine or feminine – for example, "boy" is masculine (*der Junge*). But some words are surprising – in German, "girl" is neuter (*das Mädchen*). So you should always check in the dictionary.

Finding a German word

All the German words in this book are listed at the back in the order of the alphabet. Can you put these fruits into alphabetical order?

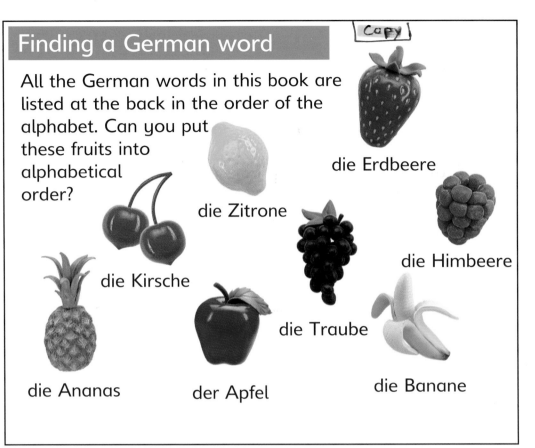

die Erdbeere

die Zitrone

die Himbeere

die Kirsche

die Traube

die Ananas

der Apfel

die Banane

Answer: die Ananas, der Apfel, die Banane, die Erdbeere, die Himbeere, die Kirsche, die Traube, die Zitrone.

Looking at a word

When you look up a word, here are some of the things you can find out.

These words in parentheses show that you can use the word in different ways.

You can check how to spell the word in English.

know   (people)   kennen,
         (facts)   wissen

Sam knows these children.
Sam kennt diese Kinder.

I know it's raining.
Ich weiß, dass es regnet.

You can see how you might use the word in English and in German.

If the word can be used in different ways, there are different phrases or sentences.

If the word can be used in different ways, there may be more than one German translation.

You can see a picture of the word, or a way of using the word.

Plurals

"Plural" means "more than one." The German for "the" when you are talking about more than one is *die* for masculine, feminine and neuter nouns. Usually, you need to change the spelling of the noun as well:

dog	der Hund
dogs	die Hunde
cat	die Katze
cats	die Katzen
house	das Haus
houses	die Häuser

You can see the plural spelling of all the words in this book in the German word list on pages 104 to 111.*

* In the word list, most nouns are written like this: *der Hund (-e)*. This means that the plural spelling of this word is *Hunde*. The plural spelling of some words is shown in full, like this: *das Haus (Häuser)*.

Nouns

In English, nouns always stay the same, no matter what part they play in a sentence. Look at the words "the dog" in these two sentences:

The dog sees Jack.

Jack sees the dog.

It doesn't matter whether the dog is seeing or being seen, its spelling doesn't change. German is different:

Der Hund sieht Jack.

Jack sieht den Hund.

Can you see how the word *der* changes to *den*? In German, the word for "the" (*der*, *die* or *das*) often changes depending on what part a noun plays in a sentence. The same thing happens with the word for "a" (*ein* for masculine and neuter nouns, *eine* for feminine nouns):

A dog has four legs.
Ein Hund hat vier Beine.

Polly has a dog.
Polly hat einen Hund.

A few masculine nouns actually change the way they are spelled. The German word for "name" is *der Name*, but it often adds an "n" on the end:

Write down your name.
Schreib deinen Namen hin.

Here are some other nouns that do the same thing:

Mr.	Herr
neighbor	der Nachbar

Adjectives

"Describing" words, such as "small" or "expensive," are called adjectives. In German, when an adjective comes before a noun, you need to add an ending to it. You add "er" with masculine nouns, "e" with feminine nouns, "es" with neuter nouns, and "e" with plural nouns:

a big tree
ein großer Baum

a green jacket
eine grüne Jacke

a cute kitten
ein niedliches Kätzchen

new shoes
neue Schuhe

You will sometimes see other adjective endings. This is because the endings change depending on what part a noun and its adjective play in the sentence:

Renata is wearing a red coat.
Renata trägt einen roten Mantel.

If an adjective comes after the noun it describes, you don't need to add any endings:

The sky is blue.
Der Himmel ist blau.

This bed is comfortable.
Dieses Bett ist bequem.

A few adjectives, such as *rosa* (pink), never add any endings:

a pink dress	ein rosa Kleid
a pink door	eine rosa Tür

Verbs

"Doing" words, such as "walk" or "laugh," are called verbs. In English, verbs don't change very much, whoever is doing them:

I walk, you walk, he walks

In German, the endings change much more. Most verbs work in a similar way to the one below. The verb is in the present – the form that you use to talk about what is happening now.

to play	spielen
I play	ich spiele
you play*	du spielst
he plays	er spielt
she plays	sie spielt
it plays	es spielt
we play	wir spielen
you play*	ihr spielt
they play	sie spielen
you play*	Sie spielen

In the main part of the dictionary, you will find each verb listed in the "to" form. You can find out more about verbs on page 99. And on pages 100 to 103, you will find a list of all the verbs in the book.

* In German, you use the *du* form for one person, either a young person or someone you know very well. You use *ihr* for more than one person that you know very well. You use *Sie* for one or more people who are older than you, or that you don't know very well. It is more polite.

4

Aa   actor *to* ambulance

actor — der Schauspieler / die Schauspielerin

The actors are waving. Die Schauspieler winken.

add (things) hinzu/fügen*, (numbers) zusammen/zählen*

Polly adds 8 and 2. Polly zählt 8 und 2 zusammen.
Billy's adding some blocks to his tower. Billy fügt ein paar Klötzchen zu seinem Turm hinzu.

address — die Adresse

This is Oliver's address. Das hier ist Olivers Adresse.

Oliver Esser
Wurststraße 34
54321 Schokostadt

adult — ein Erwachsener

Minnie is a child. Her dad is an adult. Minnie ist ein Kind. Ihr Vati ist ein Erwachsener.

(to be) afraid — Angst haben

Maddy is afraid of spiders. Maddy hat Angst vor Spinnen.

after — nach

Sacha slides down after Suki. Sacha rutscht nach Suki hinunter.

Sacha

Suki

afternoon — der Nachmittag, (in the afternoon) nachmittags

three o'clock in the afternoon
drei Uhr nachmittags

(what) age? — (wie) alt?

What age is Olivia?

Olivia

Joshua

Ben

Wie alt ist Olivia?

air — die Luft

Greta's balloon goes up into the air. Gretas Luftballon steigt in die Luft.

alone — allein

Katie is alone in the bathtub. Katie ist allein in der Badewanne.

alphabet — das Alphabet

abcdefghijklm nopqrstuvwxyz

The alphabet has 26 letters. Das Alphabet hat 26 Buchstaben.

ambulance — der Krankenwagen

The ambulance is empty. Der Krankenwagen ist leer.

a b c d e f g h i j k l m n o p q r s t u v w x y z

* This is a separable verb (see page 99).   5

amount — die Menge

a large amount of pasta
eine große Menge Nudeln

ankle — der Knöchel

Your ankle joins your leg to your foot.
Der Knöchel verbindet das Bein mit dem Fuß.

apple — der Apfel

An apple is a kind of fruit.
Der Apfel ist eine Obstsorte.

angel — der Engel

a Christmas angel
ein Weihnachtsengel

answer — die Antwort, (to answer) antworten

Question: Which animal says meow?
Answer: A cat.
Frage: Welches Tier sagt miau?
Antwort: Die Katze.

arm — der Arm

This is Jack's left arm.
Das ist Jacks linker Arm.

angry — böse

Jack is angry with Pip.
Jack ist böse auf Pip.

ant — die Ameise

Ants like sugar.
Ameisen mögen Zucker.

arrive — an/kommen*

The bus arrives at nine o'clock.
Der Bus kommt um neun Uhr an.

animal — das Tier

A lion is an animal.
Der Löwe ist ein Tier.

ape — der Affe

The ape is sitting on the ground.
Der Affe sitzt auf dem Boden.

art — die Kunst

This is Sam's picture. He's good at art.
Das hier ist Sams Bild. Er ist gut in Kunst.

a b c d e f g h i j k l m n o p q r s t u v w x y z

artist **der Künstler die Künstlerin**

The artist is painting some flowers.
Die Künstlerin malt ein paar Blumen.

baby **das Baby**

The baby is smiling.
Das Baby lächelt.

bag **die Tasche, (plastic, paper) die Tüte**

all kinds of bags
allerlei Taschen

ask **fragen**

Becky is asking, "Can I have some more strawberries?"
Becky fragt: „Kann ich noch ein paar Erdbeeren haben?"

back[1] **der Rücken**

Polly is pointing to Jack's back.
Polly deutet auf Jacks Rücken.

bake **backen**

Oliver is baking some cupcakes.
Oliver backt etwas Gebäck.

(to be) asleep **schlafen**

Nicholas is fast asleep.
Nicholas schläft fest.

(at the) back[2] **hinten, (behind) hinter**

He's at the back of the bus.
Er ist hinten im Bus.

baker **der Bäcker die Bäckerin**

The baker sells fresh bread.
Der Bäcker verkauft frisches Brot.

astronaut **der Astronaut die Astronautin**

Oliver is dressed up as an astronaut.
Oliver ist als Astronaut verkleidet.

bad **schlecht, (naughty) frech, (fruit, vegetables) faul**

bad weather
schlechtes Wetter

a bad apple
ein fauler Apfel

a bad boy
ein frecher Junge

balance **balancieren**

The clown is balancing on one hand.
Der Clown balanciert auf einer Hand.

a b c d e f g h i j k l m n o p q r s t u v w x y z

(to be) bald   **eine Glatze haben**

Mr. Rogers is bald.
Herr Rogers hat eine Glatze.

ball   **der Ball**

a brightly colored ball
ein bunter Ball

ballerina   **die Balletttänzerin**

Lucy is a ballerina.

Lucy ist eine Balletttänzerin.

balloon   **der Luftballon, (hot-air) der Ballon**

a pink balloon
ein rosa Luftballon

a balloon trip
eine Ballonfahrt

banana   **die Banane**

A banana is a kind of yellow fruit.
Die Banane ist eine gelbe Obstsorte.

band   **die Band**

Polly and Marco play in a band.
Polly und Marco spielen in einer Band.

bang   **peng**

Bang! The balloon bursts.

Peng !!

Peng! Der Luftballon platzt.

bank   **die Bank**

Mr. Brand goes to the bank to get some money.
Herr Brand geht zur Bank, um Geld abzuheben.

bar   **die Stange**

an iron bar
eine Eisenstange

bare   **nackt**

Marcus is all bare and ready for his bath.
Marcus ist ganz nackt und bereit für sein Bad.

bark¹   **die Rinde**

the bark of a tree
die Baumrinde

bark²   **bellen**

Pip is barking.
Pip bellt.

Wau! Wau!

a b c d e f g h i j k l m n o p q r s t u v w x y z

barn   die Scheune

The barn is full of hay.
Die Scheune ist voll mit Heu.

bathtub   die Badewanne

The bathtub is empty.
Die Badewanne ist leer.

bear   der Bär

This bear has a brown coat.
Dieser Bär hat ein braunes Fell.

base   der Fuß

The lamp has a yellow base.
Die Lampe hat einen gelben Fuß.

beach   der Strand

They are playing on the beach.
Sie spielen am Strand.

beard   der Bart

Mr. Brown has a beard.
Herr Brown hat einen Bart.

basket   der Korb

a big, round basket
ein großer, runder Korb

beak   der Schnabel

A toucan has a big beak.
Ein Tukan hat einen großen Schnabel.

beautiful   schön

a beautiful pink cake
ein schöner rosa Kuchen

bat (animal) die Fledermaus,
(for sports) der Schläger

A bat isn't a bird.
Die Fledermaus ist kein Vogel.

a baseball bat
ein Baseballschläger

bean   die Bohne

green beans

grüne Bohnen

bed   das Bett

a comfortable bed
ein bequemes Bett

a b c d e f g h i j k l m n o p q r s t u v w x y z

bedroom   das Schlafzimmer

Ben's bedroom   Bens Schlafzimmer

before   vor

Suki slides down before Sacha.
Suki rutscht vor Sacha hinunter.

Sacha

Suki

below   unter

The kitten is below the boards.

Das Kätzchen ist unter den Brettern.

bee   die Biene

Bees make honey.
Bienen machen Honig.

begin   beginnen

Sam's beginning to fall asleep.
Sam beginnt einzuschlafen.

belt   der Gürtel

a brown belt
ein brauner Gürtel

beetle   der Käfer

Beetles have six legs.
Käfer haben sechs Beine.

behind   hinter

The kitten is behind the flowerpot.
Das Kätzchen ist hinter dem Blumentopf.

beside   neben

The kitten is beside the flowerpot.

Das Kätzchen ist neben dem Blumentopf.

beetroot   die Rote Bete

Beetroot grows underground.
Rote Bete wächst unter der Erde.

belong   gehören

The book belongs to Suzie.
Das Buch gehört Suzie.

The CD belongs to me.
Die CD gehört mir.

between   zwischen

The kitten is between the flowerpots.

Das Kätzchen ist zwischen den Blumentöpfen.

a b c d e f g h i j k l m n o p q r s t u v w x y z

b

bib   das Lätzchen

The bib has a duck on it.
Das Lätzchen hat eine Ente darauf.

bicycle   das Fahrrad

a blue bicycle   ein blaues Fahrrad

big   groß

a big elephant   ein großer Elefant

bird   der Vogel

All birds have wings.
Alle Vögel haben Flügel.

birthday   der Geburtstag

a birthday party
eine Geburtstagsfeier

bite   beißen

Jon is biting into an apple.
Jon beißt in einen Apfel.

blanket   die Decke

a warm blanket
eine warme Decke

blow   blasen

Polly is blowing out the candles.
Polly bläst die Kerzen aus.

boat   das Boot

a rowboat
ein Ruderboot

body   der Körper

some parts of the body
einige Körperteile

arm
der Arm

tummy
der Bauch

leg
das Bein

foot
der Fuß

bone   der Knochen

How many bones does Patch have?

Wie viele Knochen hat Patch?

book   das Buch

Tina is reading a book.
Tina liest ein Buch.

a **b** c d e f g h i j k l m n o p q r s t u v w x y z

boot *to* breakfast

boot   der Stiefel

Alex wears boots when it's raining.

Alex trägt Stiefel, wenn es regnet.

bottle   die Flasche

a bottle of ketchup
eine Flasche Ketchup

a bottle of water
eine Flasche Wasser

bottom¹   der Po

Jack's bottom is inside the hoop.

Jacks Po ist im Reifen.

(at the) bottom²   unten

The kitten is at the bottom of the stairs.

Das Kätzchen ist unten an der Treppe.

bowl   die Schüssel

a plastic bowl   eine Plastikschüssel

box   (big) die Kiste, (small) die Schachtel, (cardboard) der Karton

The box is open.
Der Karton ist offen.

boy   der Junge

Oliver and Robert are boys.

Oliver und Robert sind Jungen.

branch   der Zweig

two birds on a branch

zwei Vögel auf einem Zweig

brave   tapfer

Mr. Sparks is very brave.
Herr Sparks ist sehr tapfer.

bread   das Brot

a fresh loaf of bread
ein frisches Brot

break   brechen, zerbrechen, (machine) kaputt/machen*

Asha has broken the vase.
Asha hat die Vase zerbrochen.

I've broken my radio.
Ich habe mein Radio kaputt-gemacht.

breakfast   das Frühstück

a healthy breakfast
ein gesundes Frühstück

a b c d e f g h i j k l m n o p q r s t u v w x y z

breathe   **atmen**

Divers breathe underwater.

Taucher atmen unter Wasser.

brush   **die Bürste**

a hairbrush and a toothbrush
eine Haarbürste und eine
Zahnbürste

building   **das Gebäude**

This building
has ten floors.
Dieses Gebäude
hat zehn
Stockwerke.

bridge   **die Brücke**

The bus is driving over the bridge.
Der Bus fährt über die Brücke.

bucket   **der Eimer**

buckets and shovels
Eimer und Schaufeln

bump   **stoßen**

Mr. Bun is
bumping into
the dog.
Herr Bun
stößt gegen
den Hund.

bright   **(light) hell,**
(color) knall-

a bright yellow car
ein knallgelbes
Auto

The lamp makes the room bright.
Die Lampe macht das Zimmer hell.

bug   **der Käfer**

These bugs are crawling around.

Diese Käfer krabbeln herum.

burger   **der Hamburger**

a burger with cheese
ein Hamburger mit Käse

bring   **bringen**

Jack is
bringing his
letter to the
mailbox.
Jack bringt
seinen Brief
zum
Briefkasten.

build   **bauen**

Billy is building
a tower.
Billy baut
einen Turm.

burn   **brennen, verbrennen,**
(food) anbrennen lassen

Dad has burned
the burgers.
Vati hat die
Hamburger
anbrennen
lassen.

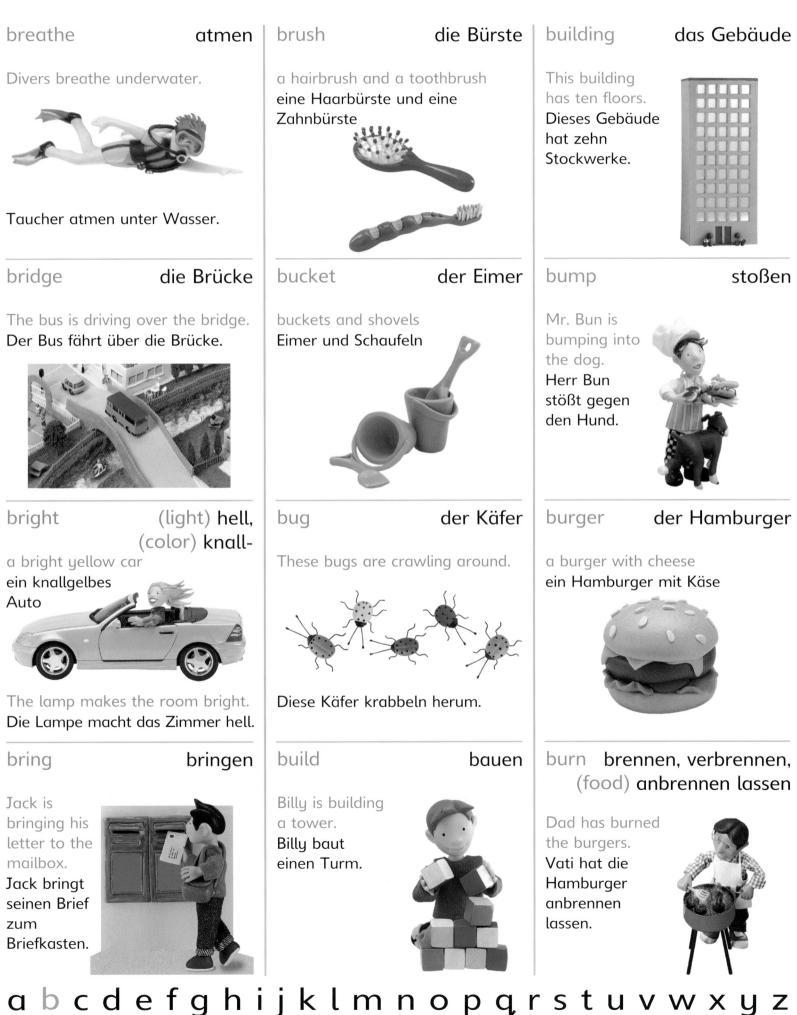

a b c d e f g h i j k l m n o p q r s t u v w x y z

bus   **der Bus**

The bus is going into town.
Der Bus fährt in die Stadt.

bush   **der Busch**

Bushes are smaller than trees.
Büsche sind kleiner als Bäume.

a tree
ein Baum

a bush
ein Busch

busy   **beschäftigt**

Mr. Bun is busy in the kitchen.
Herr Bun ist in der Küche beschäftigt.

butcher   **der Metzger**

Mrs. Beef works at the butcher's shop.
Frau Beef arbeitet beim Metzger.

butter   **die Butter**

some butter for my bread
etwas Butter für mein Brot

butterfly   **der Schmetterling**

Butterflies are insects.
Schmetterlinge sind Insekten.

button   **der Knopf**

four brightly colored buttons
vier bunte Knöpfe

buy   **kaufen**

Suzie is buying an apple.
Suzie kauft einen Apfel.

café   **das Café**

Suzie and her dad are having breakfast at the café.
Suzie und ihr Vati frühstücken im Café.

Café Weber

cage   **der Käfig**

a small cage   **ein kleiner Käfig**

cake   **der Kuchen**

a delicious cake
ein leckerer Kuchen

calf   **das Kalb**

a cow and her calf
eine Kuh und ihr Kalb

a b c d e f g h i j k l m n o p q r s t u v w x y z

call *to* castle

call (to shout) **rufen,** (to name) **nennen**

Alex is calling Pip. **Alex ruft Pip.**

Komm, Pip!

Polly calls her doll "Caroline." **Polly nennt ihre Puppe „Caroline".**

camel **das Kamel**

Camels live in the desert. **Kamele leben in der Wüste.**

camera **der Fotoapparat**

a new camera **ein neuer Fotoapparat**

camp **zelten**

They are camping. **Sie zelten.**

candle **die Kerze**

a cake with eight candles **ein Kuchen mit acht Kerzen**

cap **die Mütze**

a baseball cap **eine Baseballmütze**

car **das Auto, der Wagen**

a sports car **ein Sportwagen**

card **die Karte**

three birthday cards **drei Geburtstagskarten**

carpet **der Teppichboden, (rug) der Teppich**

My room has blue carpet.

Mein Zimmer hat einen blauen Teppichboden.

carrot **die Karotte**

A carrot is a kind of vegetable. **Die Karotte ist eine Gemüsesorte.**

carry **tragen**

Aggie is carrying some flowers. **Aggie trägt ein paar Blumen.**

castle **das Schloss, die Burg**

an old castle **eine alte Burg**

a b c d e f g h i j k l m n o p q r s t u v w x y z

cat   **die Katze**

The cat is licking its paw.
Die Katze leckt sich die Pfote.

cave   **die Höhle**

There's a bear in this cave.
In dieser Höhle ist ein Bär.

chair   **der Stuhl**

a small, blue chair
ein kleiner, blauer Stuhl

catch   **fangen**

Jack is catching the ball.
Jack fängt den Ball.

CD   **die CD**

my favorite CD
meine Lieblings-CD

chalk   **die Kreide**

a chalk drawing
eine Kreidezeichnung

caterpillar   **die Raupe**

two caterpillars
zwei Raupen

(in the) center   **mitten**

The fruit is in the center of the table.
Das Obst ist mitten auf dem Tisch.

the town center   **die Stadtmitte**

chase   **jagen**

Polly and Jack are chasing the dogs.
Polly und Jack jagen die Hunde.

cauliflower   **der Blumenkohl**

a fresh cauliflower
ein frischer Blumenkohl

cereal   **die Getreideflocken**

I eat cereal for my breakfast.
Ich esse Getreideflocken zum Frühstück.

cheap   **billig**

Everything is cheap in this store.
Alles ist billig in diesem Geschäft.

a b c d e f g h i j k l m n o p q r s t u v w x y z

cheese   **der Käse**

Swiss cheese
Schweizer Käse

chef   **der Koch**
die Köchin

Mr. Cook is a chef.
Herr Cook
ist Koch.

cherry   **die Kirsche**

red cherries
rote Kirschen

chick   **das Küken**

This hen has
five chicks.

Diese Henne hat fünf Küken.

chicken   **das Hähnchen**

I like roast
chicken.

Ich mag Brathähnchen.

child   **das Kind**

three children   **drei Kinder**

chin   **das Kinn**

Jack's chin   **Jacks Kinn**

chocolate   **die Schokolade**

a chocolate bar
eine Tafel
Schokolade

choose   **wählen,**
aus/suchen*

Billy is choosing
between the
apple and
the cupcake.
Billy wählt
zwischen dem
Apfel und
dem Kuchen.

city   **die Großstadt,**
die Stadt

There are lots   Es gibt viele
of buildings   Gebäude in einer
in a city.   Großstadt.

the city of Berlin   **die Stadt Berlin**

class   **die Klasse**

Mr. Levy's class
Herr Levys
Klasse

classroom

das Klassenzimmer
our classroom **unser Klassenzimmer**

a b c d e f g h i j k l m n o p q r s t u v w x y z

* This is a separable verb (see page 99).

clean¹   **putzen**

Clean the glass!   Putz die Scheibe!

clean²   **sauber**

Neil's clothes are clean.
Neils Kleider sind sauber.

climb   **hinauf/steigen***

Mr. Sparks is climbing the ladder to rescue the cat.
Herr Sparks steigt die Leiter hinauf, um die Katze zu retten.

clock   **die Uhr,**
(alarm clock) der Wecker

My alarm clock is very noisy.
Mein Wecker ist sehr laut.

close¹   **schließen, zu/machen***

Danny is closing the door.
Danny schließt die Tür *or* Danny macht die Tür zu.

close²   **nahe, in der Nähe**

Bill is standing close to Ben.
Bill steht nahe bei Ben.

The post office is really close.
Die Post ist ganz in der Nähe.

clothes   **die Kleider**

new clothes
neue Kleider

cloud   **die Wolke**

a big, white cloud
eine große, weiße Wolke

clown   **der Clown**

Look, the clown is juggling.
Schau mal, der Clown jongliert.

coat   **der Mantel**

Renata is wearing a red coat.
Renata trägt einen roten Mantel.

coffee   **der Kaffee**

Coffee has a strong taste.
Kaffee hat einen starken Geschmack.

coin   **die Münze**

Pete has two coins in his hand.
Pete hat zwei Münzen in der Hand.

a b c d e f g h i j k l m n o p q r s t u v w x y z

cold *to* crash

cold¹ — **die Erkältung, der Schnupfen**

Helen has a cold.
Helen hat eine Erkältung.

come — **kommen**

The clown is coming to my party.
Der Clown kommt zu meiner Party.

country¹ — **das Land**

The map shows the countries of Africa.
Die Karte zeigt die Länder von Afrika.

cold² — **kalt**

It's cold today. Ash is wearing his gloves.
Es ist kalt heute. Ash trägt seine Handschuhe.

computer — **der Computer**

a new computer
ein neuer Computer

country² — **das Land**

springtime in the country

Frühling auf dem Land

color — **die Farbe**

bright colors — bunte Farben

red — rot
green — grün
blue — blau
yellow — gelb

cook — **kochen**

Dad loves cooking.
Vati kocht sehr gern.

cow — **die Kuh**

Cows give milk.
Kühe geben Milch.

comb — **der Kamm**

a plastic comb
ein Plastikkamm

copy (actions) **nach/ahmen***, (writing) **ab/schreiben***

Sally's copying what Polly's doing.
Sally ahmt nach, was Polly macht.

crash — **gegen . . . fahren, einen Unfall haben**

The car has crashed into the tree.
Das Auto ist gegen den Baum gefahren.
Dad has crashed the car.
Vati hat einen Autounfall gehabt.

a b c d e f g h i j k l m n o p q r s t u v w x y z

* This is a separable verb (see page 99).

crawl   kriechen, (baby) krabbeln

This baby is crawling.   Dieses Baby krabbelt.

Crawl through here!   Kriech hier durch!

crayon   der Wachsmalstift

a box of crayons
eine Schachtel Wachsmalstifte

creep   schleichen

Anna is creeping into the kitchen.

Anna schleicht in die Küche.

crocodile   das Krokodil

Crocodiles live near water.
Krokodile leben nahe am Wasser.

cross¹   das Kreuz

A cross is made up of two lines.

Ein Kreuz besteht aus zwei Linien.

cross²   überqueren

a good place to cross the street

eine gute Stelle, um die Straße zu überqueren

crown   die Krone

Kings and queens wear crowns.
Könige und Königinnen tragen Kronen.

cry   weinen

Ross is crying.
Ross weint.

cucumber   die Gurke

some slices of cucumber

ein paar Scheiben Gurke

cup   die Tasse

a green cup
eine grüne Tasse

cut   schneiden, (cut out) aus/schneiden*

Danny is cutting a circle. Danny schneidet einen Kreis aus.

Cut the apple into four pieces. Schneide den Apfel in vier Teile.

cycle   mit dem Rad fahren

Sara cycles to school. Sara fährt mit dem Rad zur Schule.

a b c d e f g h i j k l m n o p q r s t u v w x y z

dance   tanzen

Stef and Laura are dancing.
Stef und Laura tanzen.

day   der Tag

The sun rises every day.

Die Sonne geht jeden Tag auf.

delicious   lecker

Jack's sandwich is delicious.
Jacks Sandwich ist lecker.

---

dangerous   gefährlich

Some snakes are dangerous.

Manche Schlangen sind gefährlich.

dear   lieber *or* liebe

Liebe Julia,
vielen Dank für die Einladung zu deiner Party am 26. August.
Ich komme gerne.
Olivia

Lieber Philipp,
vielen Dank f...
schöne Ges...
du mir zun...

dentist   der Zahnarzt
die Zahnärztin

The dentist is looking at Dad's teeth.
Der Zahnarzt sieht sich Vatis Zähne an.

---

dark   dunkel

It's dark already.
Es ist schon dunkel.

dark blue
dunkelblau

deep   tief

a deep hole
ein tiefes Loch

desert   die Wüste

a hot, dry desert
eine heiße, trockene Wüste

---

date   das Datum

What's the date today?

Januar

Welches Datum haben wir heute?

deer   der Hirsch

This deer has big horns.
Dieser Hirsch hat ein großes Geweih.

desk   der Schreibtisch

My desk has six drawers.
Mein Schreibtisch hat sechs Schubladen.

a b c **d** e f g h i j k l m n o p q r s t u v w x y z

dictionary das Wörterbuch

A dictionary explains what words mean.
Ein Wörterbuch erklärt, was Wörter bedeuten.

PICTURE DICTIONARY

dig graben

Anna is digging a hole.
Anna gräbt ein Loch.

dirty schmutzig

Sally's clothes are very dirty.
Sallys Kleider sind sehr schmutzig.

die sterben

My plant is dying because of the heat.
Meine Pflanze stirbt wegen der Hitze.

digger der Bagger

a big, yellow digger
ein großer, gelber Bagger

disappear verschwinden

Polly's dog has disappeared.
Pollys Hund ist verschwunden.

different verschieden

The twins wear different colors.
Die Zwillinge tragen verschiedene Farben.

dinner das Abendessen

Max is eating his dinner.
Max isst sein Abendessen.

dive (into water) springen, (underwater) tauchen

Jack is diving into the water.
Jack springt ins Wasser.

I like going diving.
Ich gehe gern tauchen.

difficult schwer, schwierig

It's difficult to take care of two babies at the same time.
Es ist schwer, sich um zwei Babys gleichzeitig zu kümmern.

dinosaur der Dinosaurier

an enormous dinosaur
ein riesiger Dinosaurier

diver der Taucher

The diver is looking for coral.
Der Taucher sucht nach Korallen.

a b c d e f g h i j k l m n o p q r s t u v w x y z

do — machen, tun

I have nothing to do.
Ich habe nichts zu tun.

Jenny is doing a jigsaw puzzle.
Jenny macht ein Puzzle.

doctor — der Arzt, die Ärztin

The doctor is taking care of Kirsty.
Der Arzt kümmert sich um Kirsty.

dog — der Hund

a nice dog — ein lieber Hund

doll — die Puppe

What's your doll called?
Wie heißt deine Puppe?

dolphin — der Delphin

A dolphin isn't a fish.
Der Delphin ist kein Fisch.

donkey — der Esel

A donkey looks like a small horse.
Ein Esel sieht wie ein kleines Pferd aus.

door — die Tür

The front door is red.
Die Haustür ist rot.

down — hinunter, herunter

This arrow points down.
Dieser Pfeil zeigt hinunter.

Come down!
Komm herunter!

dragon — der Drache

A dragon is a fairy-tale animal.
Der Drache ist ein Fabelwesen.

draw — zeichnen

Molly is drawing a face.
Molly zeichnet ein Gesicht.

drawing — die Zeichnung

Molly's drawing
Mollys Zeichnung

dream — der Traum, (to dream) träumen

Adam is having a strange dream.
Adam hat einen seltsamen Traum.

a b c **d** e f g h i j k l m n o p q r s t u v w x y z

dress¹　　　　das Kleid

Anya is wearing a red dress with white flowers.
Anya trägt ein rotes Kleid mit weißen Blumen.

dress²　　an/ziehen*, (yourself) sich an/ziehen*

Robert is dressing himself.
Robert zieht sich an.

I'm dressing my doll.
Ich ziehe meine Puppe an.

drink　　das Getränk, (to drink) trinken

Polly is drinking orange juice.
Polly trinkt Orangensaft.

a cold drink
ein kaltes Getränk

drive　　　　fahren

Mick is driving a dump truck.
Mick fährt einen Kipper.

drop¹　　　der Tropfen

two drops of water
zwei Wassertropfen

drop²　　fallen lassen

Ellie has dropped her cake.
Ellie hat ihren Kuchen fallen lassen.

drum　　die Trommel

a red drum　eine rote Trommel

dry¹　　trocknen, (yourself) sich ab/trocknen*

Anna is drying herself with a blue towel.
Anna trocknet sich mit einem blauen Handtuch ab.

dry²　　　　trocken

The laundry is dry.
Die Wäsche ist trocken.

duck　　die Ente

There's a duck on the water.
Auf dem Wasser ist eine Ente.

duckling　das Entenküken

How many ducklings can you see?
Wie viele Entenküken siehst du?

dull　　(color) matt, (story) langweilig

dull green
mattgrün

a dull book
ein langweiliges Buch

a b c **d** e f g h i j k l m n o p q r s t u v w x y z

Ee eagle *to* email

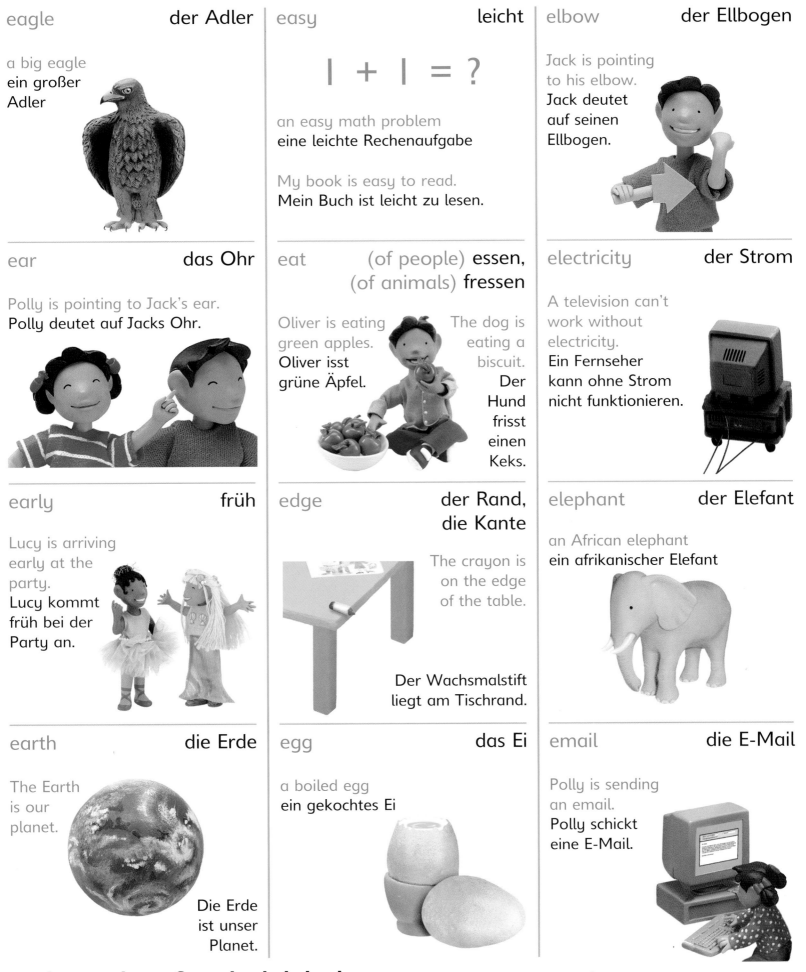

eagle — der Adler

a big eagle
ein großer
Adler

easy — leicht

| + | = ?

an easy math problem
eine leichte Rechenaufgabe

My book is easy to read.
Mein Buch ist leicht zu lesen.

elbow — der Ellbogen

Jack is pointing
to his elbow.
Jack deutet
auf seinen
Ellbogen.

ear — das Ohr

Polly is pointing to Jack's ear.
Polly deutet auf Jacks Ohr.

eat — (of people) essen,
(of animals) fressen

Oliver is eating
green apples.
Oliver isst
grüne Äpfel.

The dog is
eating a
biscuit.
Der
Hund
frisst
einen
Keks.

electricity — der Strom

A television can't
work without
electricity.
Ein Fernseher
kann ohne Strom
nicht funktionieren.

early — früh

Lucy is arriving
early at the
party.
Lucy kommt
früh bei der
Party an.

edge — der Rand,
die Kante

The crayon is
on the edge
of the table.

Der Wachsmalstift
liegt am Tischrand.

elephant — der Elefant

an African elephant
ein afrikanischer Elefant

earth — die Erde

The Earth
is our
planet.

Die Erde
ist unser
Planet.

egg — das Ei

a boiled egg
ein gekochtes Ei

email — die E-Mail

Polly is sending
an email.
Polly schickt
eine E-Mail.

a b c d e f g h i j k l m n o p q r s t u v w x y z

empty   **leer**

The cookie jar is empty.

Die Keksdose ist leer.

end   **das Ende**

ENDE

The End

enjoy   (activity) . . . **gern*,**
(yourself) **sich amüsieren**

Molly enjoys singing.
Molly singt gern.
She's enjoying herself.
Sie amüsiert sich.

enormous   **riesig**

an enormous whale
ein riesiger Wal

envelope   **der Umschlag**

a pale green envelope

ein hellgrüner Umschlag

equal   **gleich**

The two girls have equal amounts of sand.

Die zwei Mädchen haben gleich viel Sand.

escape   **entkommen**

The black cat is escaping.
Die schwarze Katze entkommt.

even   **gerade**

The pink bunny is jumping on the even numbers.
Das rosa Häschen springt auf die geraden Zahlen.

1   2   3   4   5   6   7

evening   **der Abend,**
(in the evening) **abends**
The sun sets in the evening.

Die Sonne geht abends unter.

expensive   **teuer**

The duck is cheap, but the car is quite expensive.

15

2

Die Ente ist billig, aber das Auto ist ziemlich teuer.

explain   **erklären**

Mr. Levy is explaining the math problems.

2+3 =
5+4 =
8+5 =

Herr Levy erklärt die Rechenaufgaben.

eye   **das Auge**

Jack is pointing to Polly's eye.
Jack deutet auf Pollys Auge.

a b c d e f g h i j k l m n o p q r s t u v w x y z
* Add the word *gern* after the activity you enjoy doing: I enjoy swimming. Ich schwimme gern.

face¹   das Gesicht

This is Jack's face.

Das ist Jacks Gesicht.

face²   gegenüber/stehen*

One giraffe is facing the other.

Die eine Giraffe steht der anderen gegenüber.

fact   die Tatsache

Babies sleep a lot – that's a fact.
Babys schlafen viel – das ist eine Tatsache.

fairy   die Fee

The fairy has a magic wand.

Die Fee hat einen Zauberstab.

fall   fallen, (over) hin/fallen*

Everyone laughs when the clown falls over.
Jeder lacht, wenn der Clown hinfällt.

far   weit

The butcher's shop isn't far away.

Die Metzgerei ist nicht weit weg.

farm   der Bauernhof

This farm has lots of sheep.
Dieser Bauernhof hat viele Schafe.

farmer   der Bauer

Mike is a farmer.
Mike ist Bauer.

fast   schnell

Eric goes very fast on his skis.
Eric fährt sehr schnell auf seinen Skiern.

fat   dick, fett

a fat cat
eine dicke Katze

a fat turkey
ein fetter Truthahn

feed   füttern

Polly is feeding the hens.
Polly füttert die Hühner.

feel (touch) fühlen, befühlen, (happy or sad) sich fühlen

Feel this silk!
Befühl diese Seide!

Beth is feeling great.
Beth fühlt sich toll.

a b c d e f g h i j k l m n o p q r s t u v w x y z

fence   der Zaun

the garden fence
der Gartenzaun

few   wenige

Becky has very
few strawberries.
Becky hat sehr
wenige Erdbeeren.

field   (for crops) das Feld,
(for animals) die Weide

a field with   eine Weide mit
cows in it   Kühen darauf

a corn field   ein Kornfeld

fight   kämpfen,
sich schlagen mit

The children are fighting with
cushions.
Die Kinder schlagen sich mit
Kissen.

fill   füllen

Ivan fills his wheelbarrow
with sand.
Ivan füllt seine
Schubkarre
mit Sand.

find   finden

Megan is finding
crayons under
the table.

Megan findet
Wachsmalstifte
unter dem Tisch.

finger   der Finger

Jack is pointing
to his finger.
Jack deutet
auf seinen
Finger.

finish   fertig machen,
(to have finished) fertig sein

Danny has almost
finished his juice.
Danny ist mit
seinem Saft
fast fertig.

Finish your work!
Mach deine
Arbeit fertig!

fire   das Feuer

a wood fire
ein Holzfeuer

fire engine   das Feuerwehrauto

a model fire engine
ein Modellfeuerwehrauto

firefighter der Feuerwehrmann
die Feuerwehrfrau

A firefighter
puts out
fires.

Ein
Feuerwehrmann
löscht Feuer.

first   zuerst,
erst-*

Jenny
is first.
Jenny
kommt
zuerst.

the first
door on
the left
die erste
Tür links

a b c d e **f** g h i j k l m n o p q r s t u v w x y z
* You need to add an adjective ending to this word (see page 4).

fish *to* flower

fish¹   der Fisch

I have some tropical fish.
Ich habe ein paar tropische Fische.

fish²   angeln

Karl likes fishing.
Karl angelt gern.

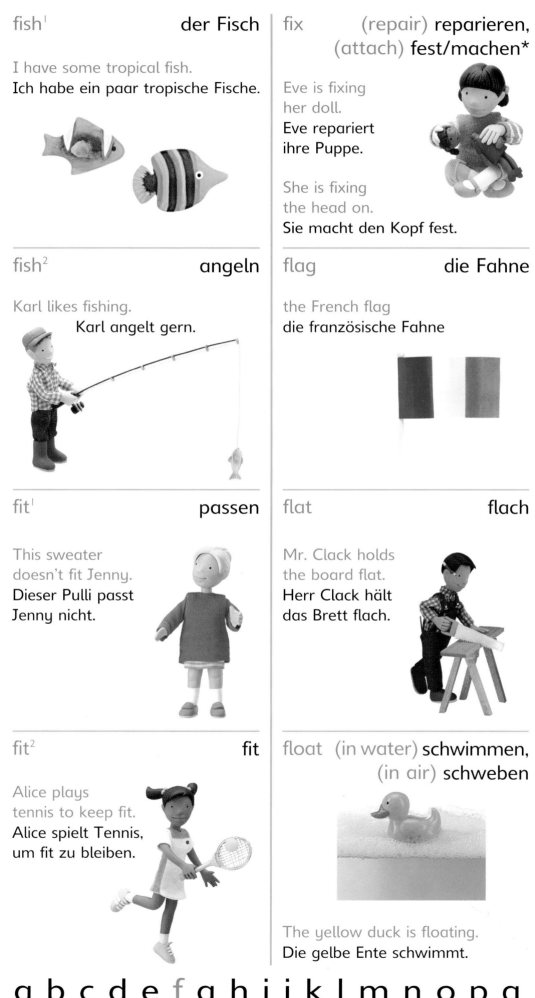

fit¹   passen

This sweater doesn't fit Jenny.
Dieser Pulli passt Jenny nicht.

fit²   fit

Alice plays tennis to keep fit.
Alice spielt Tennis, um fit zu bleiben.

fix   (repair) reparieren, (attach) fest/machen*

Eve is fixing her doll.
Eve repariert ihre Puppe.

She is fixing the head on.
Sie macht den Kopf fest.

flag   die Fahne

the French flag
die französische Fahne

flat   flach

Mr. Clack holds the board flat.
Herr Clack hält das Brett flach.

float   (in water) schwimmen, (in air) schweben

The yellow duck is floating.
Die gelbe Ente schwimmt.

flood   die Überschwemmung

There are often floods here.
Hier sind oft Überschwemmungen.

floor   der Boden

The floor is covered in toys.

Der Boden ist voller Spielsachen.

flour   das Mehl

You need flour to make bread.
Man braucht Mehl, um Brot zu backen.

flower   die Blume

Roses are my favorite flowers.

Rosen sind meine Lieblingsblumen.

a b c d e **f** g h i j k l m n o p q r s t u v w x y z

* This is a separable verb (see page 99).   29

fly¹   **die Fliege**

A fly is an insect.
**Die Fliege ist
ein Insekt.**

fly²   **fliegen**

These two birds
are flying.
**Die beiden Vögel
fliegen.**

foal   **das Fohlen**

The foal is on
the left.

Das Fohlen steht links.

fold   **zusammen/falten***

Clive is folding
the paper.
**Clive faltet
das Papier
zusammen.**

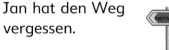

food   (prepared) **das Essen,**
(groceries) **die Lebensmittel**

lots of food for the party

viel Essen für die Party

foot   **der Fuß**

Your foot is
at the end
of your leg.
**Der Fuß ist
am Ende
des Beins.**

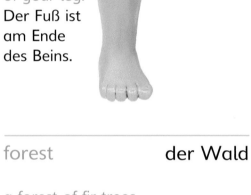

forest   **der Wald**

a forest of fir trees
ein Tannenwald

forget   **vergessen**

Jan has forgotten the way.
**Jan hat den Weg
vergessen.**

fork   **die Gabel**

a blue fork
eine blaue Gabel

fox   **der Fuchs**

This fox has red fur.
Dieser Fuchs hat ein rotes Fell.

free   (no cost) **kostenlos,
umsonst, gratis,**
(not restricted) **frei**

You can
get this
honey
free.
**Diesen
Honig
gibt es
umsonst.**

Is this space free?
Ist dieser Platz frei?

freeze   **frieren, gefrieren,**
(food) **ein/frieren***

You freeze
water to
make
ice.
**Man
gefriert
Wasser, um
Eis zu machen.**

It's
freezing
today.
Es friert heute.

a b c d e **f** g h i j k l m n o p q r s t u v w x y z

freezer der Gefrierschrank, die Tiefkühltruhe

The freezer is full. Der Gefrierschrank ist voll.

frog der Frosch

This frog is from South America. Dieser Frosch kommt aus Südamerika.

full voll, (after eating) satt

Greg's shopping cart is full. Gregs Einkaufswagen ist voll.

I'm full. Ich bin satt.

fresh frisch

All the fruit on this stand is fresh. Das ganze Obst an diesem Stand ist frisch.

front der (die, das) Vorder-*, die Vorderseite

The front door is open. Die Vordertür ist offen.

the front of the house die Vorderseite des Hauses

fun der Spaß

It's fun playing on the merry-go-round. Es macht Spaß, auf dem Karussell zu spielen.

friend der Freund die Freundin

Ellie's friends are coming to her party. Ellies Freunde kommen zu ihrer Party.

fruit das Obst

some fresh fruit etwas frisches Obst

funny (amusing) lustig, (strange) komisch

Jack is telling a funny story. Jack erzählt eine lustige Geschichte.

a funny smell ein komischer Geruch

friendly freundlich, lieb, nett

Marco is very friendly. Marco ist sehr nett.

fry braten, (an egg) ein Spiegelei machen

Daddy is frying some eggs. Vati macht Spiegeleier.

Can you fry the sausages? Kannst du die Würste braten?

fur (on animals) das Fell, (on clothes) der Pelz

This kitten has soft fur. Dieses Kätzchen hat ein weiches Fell.

a fur cap eine Pelzmütze

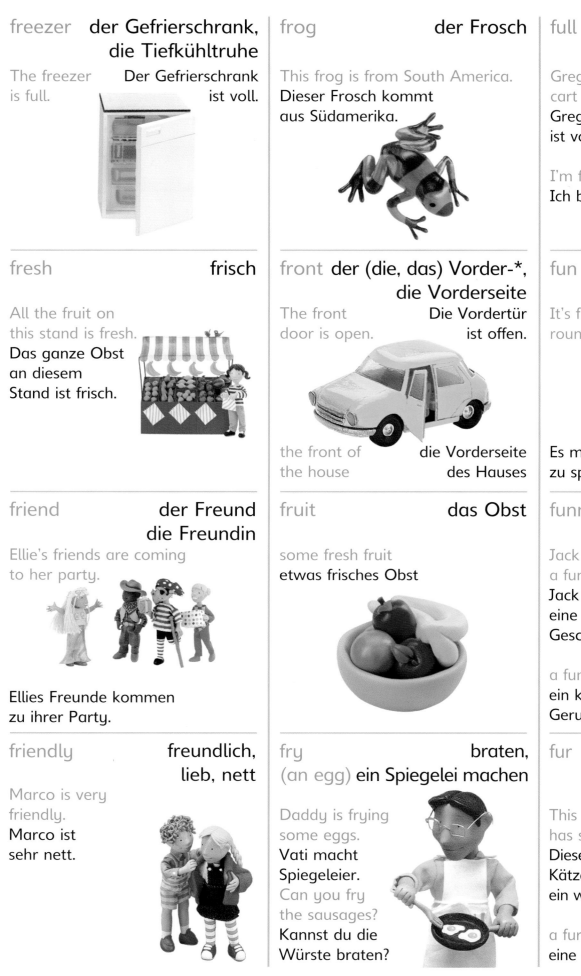

a b c d e f g h i j k l m n o p q r s t u v w x y z

* You need to join this word onto the front of the thing you're describing: the front wheel – das Vorderrad.

Gg   game *to* give

game   das Spiel

a game of basketball
ein Basketballspiel

gentle   sanft

Pip is a gentle dog.
Pip ist ein sanfter
Hund.

gift   das Geschenk

Becky has a
birthday gift
for Polly.

Becky hat ein
Geburtstagsgeschenk
für Polly.

garden   der Garten

There are lots
of flowers in
Aggie's garden.
Es gibt viele
Blumen in
Aggies Garten.

gerbil   die Wüstenspringmaus

A gerbil is a small animal.
Die Wüstenspringmaus ist
ein kleines
Tier.

giraffe   die Giraffe

A giraffe is an African animal.
Die Giraffe
ist ein
afrikanisches
Tier.

gas   das Gas

This balloon is
filled with gas.
Dieser
Luftballon
ist mit Gas
gefüllt.

ghost   das Gespenst

I don't believe
in ghosts.

Ich glaube
nicht an
Gespenster.

girl   das Mädchen

three girls   drei Mädchen

gate   das Tor

The garden gate is blue.
Das Gartentor ist blau.

giant   der Riese

a friendly
giant

ein freundlicher
Riese

give   geben,
(as a gift) schenken

Ethan is
giving
Jenny
some
wagons.

Ethan gibt Jenny
ein paar Waggons.

a b c d e f **g** h i j k l m n o p q r s t u v w x y z

glad *to* goose

(to be) glad — **sich freuen**

Sally is glad to see Jenny.
Sally freut sich, Jenny zu sehen.

glass — **das Glas**

Windows are made of glass.
Fenster sind aus Glas.

a glass of milk
ein Glas Milch

glasses — **die Brille**

Dad and Granny wear glasses.
Vati und Oma tragen eine Brille.

glove — **der Handschuh**

Polly has a pair of red gloves.
Polly hat ein Paar rote Handschuhe.

glue — **der Klebstoff**

Danny is making a picture with paper and glue.
Danny macht ein Bild aus Papier und Klebstoff.

go — **(on foot) gehen, (by car, boat, train) fahren**

The cars are going into the ferry.

Die Autos fahren in die Fähre hinein.

goal — **das Tor**

Our team has scored a goal.
Unsere Mannschaft hat ein Tor geschossen.

TOR!

goat — **die Ziege**

Goats climb hills very well.
Ziegen klettern sehr gut auf Berge.

gold — **das Gold, (golden) golden**

Gold is a precious metal.
a gold watch
eine goldene Uhr

Gold ist ein Edelmetall.

good — **gut, (well-behaved) artig, brav**

a good meal
ein gutes Essen

Good work!
Gute Arbeit!

3 + 3 = 6 ✓
2 + 5 = 7 ✓
8 - 6 = 2 ✓
4 + 1 = 5 ✓

a good child
ein braves Kind

goodbye — **auf Wiedersehen, (to say goodbye) sich verabschieden**

Polly is saying goodbye to her friends.
Polly verabschiedet sich von ihren Freunden.

Auf Wiedersehen!

goose — **die Gans**

A goose is a bird with a long neck.
Eine Gans ist ein Vogel mit einem langen Hals.

a b c d e f **g** h i j k l m n o p q r s t u v w x y z

grape   die Traube

a bunch of grapes
ein Bund Trauben

ground   der Boden

Polly is looking at ants on the ground.
Polly schaut sich Ameisen auf dem Boden an.

guess   raten

Can you guess what Polly's present is?
Kannst du raten, was Pollys Geschenk ist?

grapefruit   die Grapefruit

I like grapefruit with sugar.
Ich mag Grapefruit mit Zucker.

group   die Gruppe

a group of children
eine Gruppe Kinder

guest   der Gast

Ellie is welcoming the guests.
Ellie begrüßt die Gäste.

grass   das Gras

Cows and sheep eat grass.
Kühe und Schafe fressen Gras.

grow (get bigger) **wachsen,** (cultivate) **ziehen**

My plant is growing very fast.
Meine Pflanze wächst sehr schnell.

We grow vegetables in our garden.
Wir ziehen Gemüse in unserem Garten.

guinea pig   das Meerschweinchen

a cute guinea pig
ein niedliches Meerschweinchen

great   (big) **groß,** (fantastic) **toll**

a great success
ein großer Erfolg

a great day on the beach
ein toller Tag am Strand

grown-up   der Erwachsene

Grown-ups are always stopping to talk.
Erwachsene bleiben ständig stehen, um sich zu unterhalten.

guitar   die Gitarre

an electric guitar
eine elektrische Gitarre

a b c d e f **g** h i j k l m n o p q r s t u v w x y z

hair   die Haare

Rosie and Katie have fair hair.

Rosie und Katie haben blonde Haare.

hairbrush   die Haarbürste

I have a red hairbrush.
Ich habe eine rote Haarbürste.

half   halb, (portion) die Hälfte

two-and-a-half hours
zweieinhalb Stunden

half the bun
die Brötchenhälfte

hamburger   der Hamburger

a hamburger with cheese

ein Hamburger mit Käse

hammer   der Hammer

a hammer for doing carpentry

ein Hammer zum Heimwerken

hamster   der Hamster

Hamsters eat nuts and seeds.
Hamster fressen Nüsse und Samen.

hand   die Hand

This is Jack's left hand.
Das ist Jacks linke Hand.

handle   der Griff, (door) die Klinke, (pan) der Stiel

the door handle   die Türklinke

The pan handle's broken.
Der Pfannenstiel ist kaputt.

hang   hängen

Jack is hanging his jacket up.
Jack hängt seine Jacke auf.

happen   passieren, los sein

What's happening here?
Was ist hier los?

happy   glücklich

Sally is feeling very happy today.
Sally ist heute sehr glücklich.

hard   (surface) hart, (task) schwer, schwierig

It can be hard putting up a tent.
Es kann schwer sein, ein Zelt aufzuschlagen.

The ground is hard.
Der Boden ist hart.

a b c d e f g **h** i j k l m n o p q r s t u v w x y z

hat *to* helmet

hat   **der Hut**

an orange hat with a flower on it   ein orangefarbener Hut mit einer Blume darauf

hate   **hassen, nicht leiden können**

It's wrong to hate other people.
Es ist unrecht, andere Menschen zu hassen.

Maddy hates spiders.
Maddy kann Spinnen nicht leiden.

have   **haben**

Julia has some new red shoes.
Julia hat neue rote Schuhe.

head   **der Kopf**

Polly's head is in the hoop.
Pollys Kopf ist im Reifen.

hear   **hören**

Jack can hear the dog barking.

Wau! Wau!

Jack hört den Hund bellen.

heart   **das Herz**

My heart is beating fast.
Mein Herz schlägt schnell.

heart shaped
herzförmig

heat   (food) **auf/wärmen*,** (a room) **heizen**

Yvonne is heating her coffee in the microwave.
Yvonne wärmt ihren Kaffee in der Mikrowelle auf.

heavy   **schwer**

The package is too heavy.

Das Paket ist zu schwer.

height   (person) **die Größe,** (house, mountain) **die Höhe**

We're flying at a height of 30,000ft.
Wir fliegen in einer Höhe von 9000m.

What height is Milo?
Wie groß ist Milo?**

helicopter   **der Hubschrauber**

a rescue helicopter
ein Rettungshubschrauber

hello   **hallo**

Lisa is saying hello to her sister.

Hallo!

Lisa sagt ihrer Schwester „Hallo!"

helmet   **der Helm**

Grace wears a helmet for skateboarding.
Grace trägt einen Helm beim Skateboardfahren.

a b c d e f g **h** i j k l m n o p q r s t u v w x y z

help   **helfen**

Jack is helping
his dad with
the cooking.
Jack hilft
seinem Vati
beim Kochen.

hen   **das Huhn,**
die Henne

Hens lay
eggs.

Hühner
legen Eier.

hide   (things) **verstecken,**
(yourself) **sich verstecken**

The clown is
hiding behind
the armchair.
Der Clown
versteckt sich
hinter dem Sessel.

high   **hoch,**
(before a noun) **hoh-***

The balloon
is floating high
in the sky.
Der Ballon
schwebt hoch
am Himmel.

a high building
ein hohes Gebäude

highchair   **der Hochstuhl**

Highchairs
are for
small
children.
Hochstühle
sind für
kleine
Kinder.

hill   **der Hügel**

Our house is at the top of a hill.
Unser Haus ist oben
auf einem Hügel.

hippopotamus
or **hippo**   **das Nilpferd**

Hippos live
in Africa.

Nilpferde
leben in Afrika.

hit   **schlagen**

Alice is hitting the ball
with her racket.
Alice schlägt
den Ball mit
ihrem Schläger.

hold   **halten**

Neil is holding
the trophy.
Neil hält
den Pokal.

hole   **das Loch**

This
sweater
has a hole in it.
Dieser Pulli hat ein Loch.

home   **das Haus,**
This is our
home.
(at home) **zu Hause**

Das ist unser Haus.

honey   **der Honig**

Honey is
very sweet.
Honig ist
sehr süß.

* You need to add an adjective ending to this word (see page 4).

hop — **hüpfen**

Anna is hopping on one leg.
Anna hüpft auf einem Bein.

hotdog — **der Hotdog**

A hotdog is a sausage in a bun.
Ein Hotdog ist eine Wurst in einem Brötchen.

hug — (person) **umarmen,** (toy, animal) **an sich drücken**

Nicholas is hugging his teddy bear.
Nicholas drückt seinen Teddy an sich.

horse — **das Pferd**

Martin likes riding his horse.
Martin reitet gern auf seinem Pferd.

hotel — **das Hotel**

Mr. Brand is spending his vacation at this hotel.
Herr Brand verbringt seinen Urlaub in diesem Hotel.

HOTEL LUCIDA

(to be) hungry — **Hunger haben**

Oliver is hungry.
Oliver hat Hunger.

hospital — **das Krankenhaus**

the new hospital
das neue Krankenhaus

hour — **die Stunde**

The short hand on the clock shows the hours.
Der kurze Zeiger auf der Uhr zeigt die Stunden an.

hurry — **sich beeilen**

Jack and Polly are hurrying to catch the dog.
Jack und Polly beeilen sich, um den Hund zu fangen.

hot — **heiß**

Careful, the stove's hot!
Vorsicht, der Herd ist heiß!

house — **das Haus**

a house with a yard
ein Haus mit einem Garten

hurt — **weh/tun***

Ross is crying because his tummy hurts.
Ross weint, denn sein Bauch tut weh.

a b c d e f g **h** i j k l m n o p q r s t u v w x y z

Ii ice *to* itch

ice — das Eis

three ice cubes

drei Eiswürfel

ice cream — das Eis

different flavors of ice cream

verschiedene Eissorten

idea — die Idee

Gehen wir zum Park!

Andy has an idea: Let's go to the park!

Andy hat eine Idee.

insect — das Insekt

All insects have six legs.

Alle Insekten haben sechs Beine.

inside — in, (indoors) hinein, herein

There's a kitten inside this flowerpot.

Da ist ein Kätzchen in diesem Blumentopf.

Let's go inside.

Gehen wir hinein.

Come inside!

Komm herein!

instead (of) — statt

Ich habe heute Eistee statt Fruchtsaft gemacht.

Mrs. Dot has made iced tea instead of fruit juice today.

Internet — das Internet

Polly is searching the Internet.

Polly sucht im Internet.

invitation — die Einladung

a party invitation — eine Einladung zu einer Party

Imogen lädt dich am Samstag, den 6. April um 16.30 Uhr zu ihrer Party ein.

invite — ein/laden*

Imogen is inviting Martin to her party.

Kommst du zu meiner Party?

Imogen lädt Martin zu ihrer Party ein.

iron — das Bügeleisen, (to iron) bügeln

a steam iron

ein Dampfbügeleisen

Dad is ironing his pants.

Vati bügelt seine Hose.

island — die Insel

a desert island

eine einsame Insel

itch — jucken

Fred's ear itches.

Freds Ohr juckt.

a b c d e f g h **i** j k l m n o p q r s t u v w x y z

jacket — die Jacke

Kathy is wearing a yellow jacket.
Kathy trägt eine gelbe Jacke.

jar — das Glas

jars of honey, mustard and jelly
Gläser mit Honig, Senf und Marmelade

jeans — die Jeans

new jeans
neue Jeans

jigsaw puzzle — das Puzzle

This jigsaw puzzle is easy.
Dieses Puzzle ist leicht.

job — die Stelle, der Job

I'm looking for a job.
Ich suche eine Stelle.

Aggie has a job.
She is a gardener.
Aggie hat einen Job. Sie ist Gärtnerin.

join — (attach) verbinden, (become a member) Mitglied werden

Ethan is joining the wagons to the train.
Ethan verbindet die Waggons mit dem Zug.

I'm joining a club.
Ich werde Mitglied in einem Klub.

joke — der Witz

Jack's joke:
Jacks Witz:

Welches Tier macht sssb?

Eine Biene, die rückwärts fliegt!

What animal goes zzzub?
A bee going backward!

journey — die Fahrt, die Reise

a train journey
eine Zugfahrt

Have a good journey!
Gute Reise!

juggle — jonglieren

The clown is juggling with some toys.
Der Clown jongliert mit ein paar Spielsachen.

juice — der Saft

a glass of orange juice
ein Glas Orangensaft

jump — springen

Sally is jumping in the air.
Sally springt in die Luft.

jungle — der Dschungel

There are lots of plants and animals in the jungle.
Im Dschungel sind viele Pflanzen und Tiere.

a b c d e f g h i **j** k l m n o p q r s t u v w x y z

Kk
kangaroo *to* kite

k

kangaroo das Känguru	**kid** das Zicklein	**king** der König
A kangaroo is an Australian animal.	a goat and her kid eine Ziege und ihr Zicklein	Adam is dressed up as a king.
Das Känguru ist ein australisches Tier.		Adam ist als König verkleidet.

keep (store) auf/bewahren*, (have) behalten

Sam keeps his things on the shelf.
Sam bewahrt seine Sachen auf dem Regal auf.

Can I keep this book?
Kann ich dieses Buch behalten?

kill töten

The heat has killed my plant.

Die Hitze hat meine Pflanze getötet.

kiss der Kuss, (to kiss) küssen

Polly is kissing Alex.
Polly küsst Alex.

Give me a kiss.
Gib mir einen Kuss.

key der Schlüssel

the front door key
der Hausschlüssel

kind¹ die Sorte, die Art

different kinds of fruit
verschiedene Obstsorten

kitchen die Küche

The kitchen is on the ground floor.

Die Küche ist im Erdgeschoss.

kick kicken

Neil is kicking the ball.

Neil kickt den Ball.

kind² nett, lieb

Mr. Dot is kind. He does his neighbor's shopping.
Herr Dot ist nett. Er geht für seinen Nachbarn einkaufen.

kite der Drachen

a red and yellow kite
ein rotgelber Drachen

a b c d e f g h i j **k** l m n o p q r s t u v w x y z

* This is a separable verb (see page 99).   41

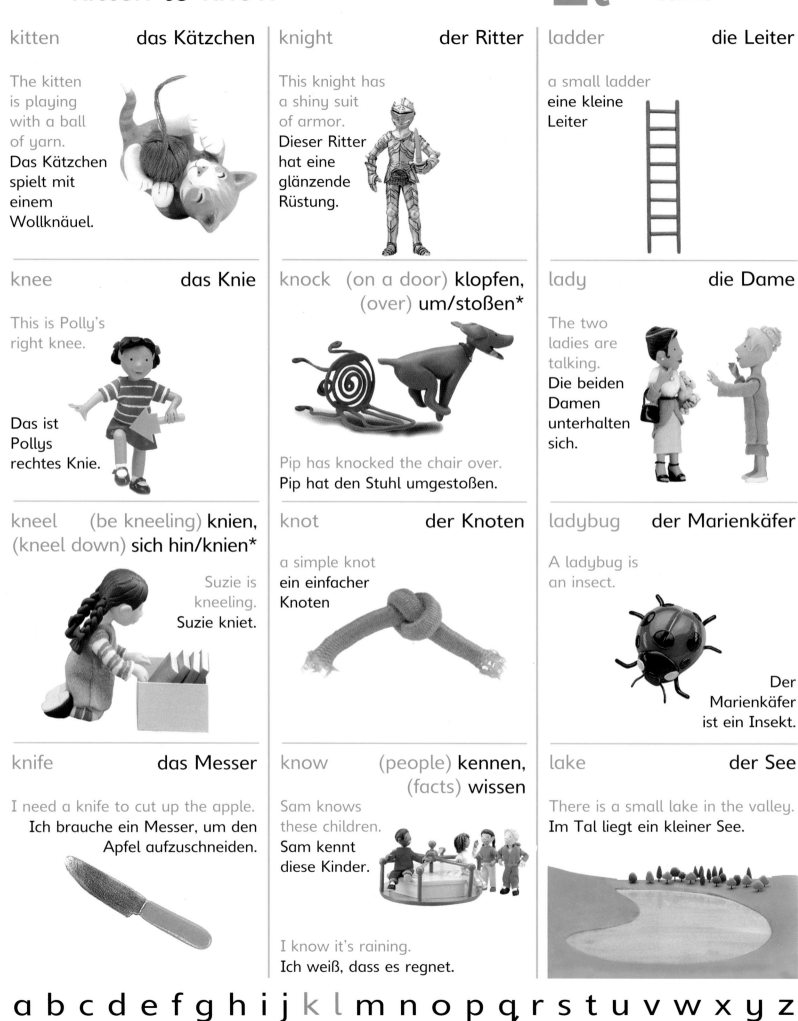

kitten   das Kätzchen

The kitten is playing with a ball of yarn.
Das Kätzchen spielt mit einem Wollknäuel.

knee   das Knie

This is Polly's right knee.
Das ist Pollys rechtes Knie.

kneel   (be kneeling) knien, (kneel down) sich hin/knien*

Suzie is kneeling.
Suzie kniet.

knife   das Messer

I need a knife to cut up the apple.
Ich brauche ein Messer, um den Apfel aufzuschneiden.

knight   der Ritter

This knight has a shiny suit of armor.
Dieser Ritter hat eine glänzende Rüstung.

knock (on a door) klopfen, (over) um/stoßen*

Pip has knocked the chair over.
Pip hat den Stuhl umgestoßen.

knot   der Knoten

a simple knot
ein einfacher Knoten

know (people) kennen, (facts) wissen

Sam knows these children.
Sam kennt diese Kinder.

I know it's raining.
Ich weiß, dass es regnet.

ladder   die Leiter

a small ladder
eine kleine Leiter

lady   die Dame

The two ladies are talking.
Die beiden Damen unterhalten sich.

ladybug   der Marienkäfer

A ladybug is an insect.
Der Marienkäfer ist ein Insekt.

lake   der See

There is a small lake in the valley.
Im Tal liegt ein kleiner See.

lamb   das Lamm

A lamb is a baby sheep.
Ein Lamm ist ein junges Schaf.

lamp   die Lampe

Here are two table lamps.
Hier sind zwei
Tischlampen.

land   das Land

On this map, the land is brown.
Auf dieser Karte
ist das Land
braun.

language   die Sprache

¡Buenos días!

Bonjour!

They can speak foreign languages.
Sie können Fremdsprachen.

large   groß

a large tree
ein großer
Baum

last   zuletzt, letzt-*

The black
dog is last.
Der schwarze
Hund kommt zuletzt.

last week   letzte Woche

late   spät

The bus always
arrives late.
Der Bus kommt
immer spät an.

I was late
for school.
Ich bin zu spät
zur Schule gekommen.

HAUPTSTRA
22

laugh   lachen

Jack and Polly are laughing.

Ha! Ha! Ha!

Hi! Hi! Hi!

Jack und
Polly
lachen.

lazy   faul

a lazy cat
eine faule Katze

lead   führen, (go in front) voran/gehen**

The white duck is leading.

Die weiße Ente geht voran.

This road leads to the village.
Diese Straße führt zum Dorf.

leaf   das Blatt

green leaves
grüne Blätter

lean (lean on) sich stützen, (to one side) sich neigen

The tower leans
to the right.
Der Turm neigt
sich nach rechts.

Lean on
my arm.
Stütz dich auf
meinen Arm.

a b c d e f g h i j k l m n o p q r s t u v w x y z

* You need to add an adjective ending to this word (see page 4).
** This is a separable verb (see page 99).

l

learn *to* lick

learn   **lernen**

Steve is learning
to play the guitar.
**Steve lernt, Gitarre
zu spielen.**

leave   (a place) **verlassen,**
(something) **liegen lassen**

Mr. Bun is
leaving the
house.
**Herr Bun
verlässt das
Haus.**

I've left my bag at home.
**Ich habe meine Tasche
zu Hause liegen lassen.**

left   **links, link-***

Turn left!
Geh nach links!
Lisa is holding
the crayon in
her left hand.
**Lisa hält den
Wachsmalstift
in der linken
Hand.**

leg   **das Bein**

Tamsin wears tights to
keep her legs warm.
**Tamsin trägt eine
Strumpfhose, um
sich die Beine
warm zu halten.**

lemon   **die Zitrone**

seven fresh
lemons

sieben
frische Zitronen

length   **die Länge**

Use a ruler to measure
the length of the paper.
**Benutze ein Lineal, um
die Länge des
Papiers zu
messen.**

less   **weniger**

Ethan has less ice cream
than Olivia.
Ethan hat weniger Eis als Olivia.

lesson   **die Stunde**

Mr. Levy is giving a math lesson.
**Herr Levy
gibt eine
Mathe-
stunde.**

$2 + 4 = 6$

let   **lassen**

Mr. Dot is letting
Jack mail the letter.
**Herr Dot
lässt Jack
den Brief
einwerfen.**

letter   **der Brief**

a letter to a friend
**ein Brief an
eine Freundin**

Eidorf, den 31. März

Liebe Anja,

*vielen Dank für die schöne
Tasche, die du mir geschenkt
hast. Ich nehme sie jeden Tag
mit zur Schule.*

Liebe Grüße,

Olivia

lettuce   **der Kopfsalat**

a fresh head of lettuce
**ein frischer
Kopfsalat**

lick   **lecken,**
(animals) **ab/lecken****

Pip is licking
Jack.

Pip leckt Jack ab.

a b c d e f g h i j k l m n o p q r s t u v w x y z

* You need to add an adjective ending to this word (see page 4).
** This is a separable verb (see page 99).

lid der Deckel

the lid of the mustard jar
der Senfglasdeckel

lie¹ (be lying) liegen, (lie down) sich hin/legen*

Kirsty is lying in bed.
Kirsty liegt im Bett.

Lie down!
Leg dich hin!

lie² lügen

He's lying.
Er lügt.

Sie ist nicht da? Nein!

life das Leben

Granny and Grandpa have had long, happy lives.
Oma und Opa haben ein langes, glückliches Leben geführt.

lift hoch/heben*

The clown is trying to lift the tree.
Der Clown versucht, den Baum hochzuheben.

light¹ das Licht

This lamp gives a lot of light.
Diese Lampe gibt viel Licht.

Turn off the light!
Mach das Licht aus!

light² (color) hell, (not heavy) leicht

a light pink beach hut
ein hellrosa Strandhäuschen

This bag is really light.
Diese Tasche ist wirklich leicht.

like¹ (activities) . . . gern**, (people, things) mögen

I like playing tennis.
Ich spiele gern Tennis.
Becky likes strawberries.
Becky mag Erdbeeren.

like² wie

Sara has black hair, like her brother.
Sara hat schwarze Haare wie ihr Bruder.

line (on paper) die Linie, (of people) die Reihe

a line of soccer players
eine Reihe Fußballspieler

Draw a line. Zeichne eine Linie.

lion der Löwe

Lions live in Africa.
Löwen leben in Afrika.

lip die Lippe

Zach's top lip
Zachs Oberlippe

a b c d e f g h i j k l m n o p q r s t u v w x y z

* This is a separable verb (see page 99). 45
** Add the word *gern* after the activity you like doing: I like singing. Ich singe gern.

list   **die Liste**

a list of first names
**eine Liste mit
Vornamen**

Adam
Becky
Danny
Ellie
Katie
Maddy
Ross
Tony

live   (in a place) **wohnen,**
      (be alive) **leben**

The Dot family lives here.
Die Familie Dot wohnt hier.

lock   **das Schloss**

I need the key for this lock.
**Ich brauche den
Schlüssel
für dieses
Schloss.**

log   **der Baumstamm,**
(for a fire) **das Holzscheit**

a log for
the fire
**ein Holzscheit
fürs Feuer**

long   **lang**

A giraffe has a
very long neck.
**Eine Giraffe hat
einen sehr
langen Hals.**

look   **an/schauen*,
an/sehen***

Polly is looking
at the clown.
**Polly schaut
den Clown an**
or **Polly sieht
den Clown an.**

lose   **verlieren**

I've lost my ticket.
**Ich habe meine
Fahrkarte verloren.**

The boys have
lost the match.
**Die Jungen
haben das
Spiel verloren.**

(a) lot   (of one thing) **viel,**
      (of things) **viele**

a lot of water
viel Wasser

a lot of
teddy
bears
**viele
Teddys**

loud   **laut**

The music is too loud.

Die Musik ist zu laut.

love   (people) **lieben,**
(things) **sehr gern mögen,**
(activities) **. . . sehr gern****

Beth   Beth
loves her   mag ihre
pink bathtub.   rosa Badewanne
            sehr gern.

low   **niedrig**

This bird is flying very low.
Dieser Vogel fliegt sehr niedrig.

lunch   **das Mittagessen**

Sally is eating   Sally isst ihr
her lunch.   Mittagessen.

a b c d e f g h i j k l m n o p q r s t u v w x y z

* This is a separable verb (see page 99).   46
** Add the words *sehr gern* after the activity you love doing: I love dancing. **Ich tanze sehr gern.**

machine — **die Maschine**

a sewing machine

eine Nähmaschine

man — **der Mann**

This man has black hair.
Dieser Mann hat schwarze Haare.

match[1] (game) **das Spiel, das Match,** (for fire) **das Streichholz**

a soccer match
ein Fußballspiel

I have one match left.
Ich habe ein Streichholz übrig.

magic — **die Zauberkunst, der (die, das) Zauber-***

The clown is doing a magic trick.
Der Clown macht ein Zauberkunststück.

a magic spell
ein Zauberspruch

many — **viele**

There are many bees on this flower.

Auf dieser Blume sind viele Bienen.

match[2] **zusammen/passen****

These socks match.
Diese Socken passen zusammen.

These socks don't match.
Diese Socken passen nicht zusammen.

main **der (die, das) Haupt-***

the main entrance of the museum
der Haupteingang des Museums

map — **die Landkarte, die Karte**

a map of the region
eine Karte des Gebiets

matter — **wichtig sein**

Winning matters a lot to Neil and his team.

Gewinnen ist für Neil und seine Mannschaft sehr wichtig.

make — **machen**

Ethan is making potato people.
Ethan macht Kartoffelmännchen.

market — **der Markt**

the fruit and vegetable market
der Obst- und Gemüsemarkt

meal — **die Mahlzeit, das Essen**

The meal is almost ready.
Das Essen ist fast fertig.

a b c d e f g h i j k l m n o p q r s t u v w x y z

* You need to join this word onto the front of the thing you're describing: a magic wand – ein Zauberstab; the main street – die Hauptstraße. ** This is a separable verb (see page 99).

mean   **bedeuten**

Mr. Levy is explaining what "x" means.
Herr Levy erklärt, was „x" bedeutet.

meet (by chance) **begegnen,** (by arrangement) **sich treffen**

I'm meeting Dad at six.
Ich treffe mich mit Vati um sechs Uhr.
Polly has met Lisa at the market.
Polly ist Lisa auf dem Markt begegnet.

metal   **das Metall**

This bucket is made of metal.
Dieser Eimer ist aus Metall.

measure   **messen**

Dad is measuring Milo's height.
Vati misst, wie groß Milo ist.

mend   **reparieren,** (clothes) **flicken**

Robert is mending his shirt.
Robert flickt sein Hemd.

microwave   **die Mikrowelle**

a new microwave
eine neue Mikrowelle

meat   **das Fleisch**

Chicken is a kind of meat.
Hähnchen ist eine Fleischsorte.

mess   **das Durcheinander,** (dirt) **der Dreck**

What a mess!
So ein Durcheinander!

middle   **die Mitte,** (in the middle) **mitten**

The bear is in the middle of the grass.
Der Bär ist mitten auf dem Gras.

the middle of the town
die Stadtmitte

medicine   **das Medikament, das Mittel**

cough medicine
ein Mittel gegen Husten

message   **die Nachricht**

There's a message for Mom to call Paula.
Da ist eine Nachricht für Mutti:

Mutti, kannst du Paula anrufen?

milk   **die Milch**

fresh milk
frische Milch

a b c d e f g h i j k l **m** n o p q r s t u v w x y z

mind	etwas gegen . . . haben, aus/machen*

I don't mind spiders.
Ich habe nichts gegen Spinnen.
I don't mind if it rains.
Es macht mir nichts aus, wenn es regnet.

minute	die Minute

It's a few minutes past nine.
Es ist ein paar Minuten nach neun.

mirror	der Spiegel

Jack's looking at himself in the mirror.
Jack schaut sich im Spiegel an.

miss	(train, bus) verpassen, (person) vermissen

Liddy misses her mom.
Liddy vermisst ihre Mutti.

Becky's missed the bus.
Becky hat den Bus verpasst.

mistake	der Fehler

I've made a spelling mistake.
Ich habe einen Schreibfehler gemacht.

Giraffe
Hubschrauber
Marienkäfer
Schokolade
Zweig

mix	mischen, (cooking) verrühren

Oliver is mixing the ingredients to make a cake.
Oliver verrührt die Zutaten, um einen Kuchen zu machen.

model	das Modell

Billy has a model boat.
Billy hat ein Modellboot.

money	das Geld

I have some money to buy a present.
Ich habe etwas Geld, um ein Geschenk zu kaufen.

monkey	der Affe

five funny monkeys
fünf lustige Affen

month	der Monat

There are twelve months in a year.
Das Jahr hat zwölf Monate.

Januar
Februar
März
April
Mai
Juni
Juli
August
September
Oktober
November
Dezember

moon	der Mond

The moon is out. Der Mond scheint.

more	mehr

Sally has more sand than Amy.

Sally   Amy

Sally hat mehr Sand als Amy.

a b c d e f g h i j k l **m** n o p q r s t u v w x y z

* This is a separable verb (see page 99). It's also the other way around from English – as though you were saying "It doesn't bother me if it rains."

m

morning   der Vormittag, der Morgen

a summer morning
ein Sommermorgen

mountain   der Berg

Mountains are higher than hills.
Berge sind höher als Hügel.

much   viel

Mrs. Moon hasn't bought much.
Frau Moon hat nicht viel gekauft.

most   meist-*

Which caterpillar has the most stripes?

Welche Raupe hat die meisten Streifen?

mouse   die Maus

a house mouse
eine Hausmaus

a computer mouse
eine Computermaus

mud   der Schlamm

Sally is covered in mud.
Sally ist voller Schlamm.

moth   der Nachtfalter

Moths come out at night.

Nachtfalter kommen nachts heraus.

mouth   der Mund

Jack is pointing to Polly's mouth.
Jack deutet auf Pollys Mund.

mushroom   der Pilz

Mushrooms grow in fields and in woods.
Pilze wachsen auf Weiden und in Wäldern.

motorcycle   das Motorrad

This is Steve's new motorcycle.

Das hier ist Steves neues Motorrad.

move (yourself) sich bewegen, **(an object)** um/stellen**

The crane is moving the crate.
Der Kran stellt die Kiste um.

Don't move!   Beweg dich nicht!

music   die Musik

Steve, Marco and Molly love music.
Steve, Marco und Molly mögen Musik sehr gern.

a b c d e f g h i j k l **m** n o p q r s t u v w x y z

* You need to add an adjective ending to this word (see page 4).
** This is a separable verb (see page 99).

Nn
nail *to* nest

nail der Nagel

I need some nails to fix the chair.
Ich brauche ein paar Nägel, um den Stuhl zu reparieren.

pink nail polish
rosa Nagellack

name der Name*

Polly is choosing a name for her tiger.
Polly sucht einen Namen für ihren Tiger aus.

narrow eng

The gap is too narrow – the kitten can't fit through.
Der Spalt ist zu eng – das Kätzchen kommt nicht durch.

nature die Natur

Polly is interested in nature.
Polly interessiert sich für die Natur.

naughty frech, unartig

That naughty dog has stolen Jack's cake.
Der freche Hund da hat Jacks Kuchen gestohlen.

near in der Nähe von

The school is near the river.
Die Schule ist in der Nähe von dem Fluss.

neck der Hals

A giraffe has a very long neck.
Eine Giraffe hat einen sehr langen Hals.

necklace die Halskette

Ruth has a pretty necklace.
Ruth hat eine hübsche Halskette.

need (something) brauchen, **(to do something)** müssen

Sam needs to sleep.
Sam muss schlafen.

I need a pencil.
Ich brauche einen Bleistift.

needle die Nadel

a sewing needle
eine Nähnadel

two red knitting needles
zwei rote Stricknadeln

neighbor der Nachbar die Nachbarin

These two people are neighbors.
Diese zwei Leute sind Nachbarn.

nest das Nest

Birds build nests for their eggs.
Vögel bauen Nester für ihre Eier.

a b c d e f g h i j k l m **n** o p q r s t u v w x y z
* You sometimes need to add an "n" on the end of this word (see page 4).

net[1] das Netz

Julia has a small fishing net.
Julia hat ein kleines Fischernetz.

The ball's in the net.
Der Ball ist im Netz.

Net[2] das Internet

Polly is searching the Net.
Polly sucht im Internet.

never nie

The mailman never smiles.
Der Briefträger lächelt nie.

new neu

Julia has some new shoes.
Julia hat neue Schuhe.

news die Nachricht, das Neueste

Mrs. Beef has some bad news: her cat is gone!
Frau Beef hat eine schlechte Nachricht:

Meine Katze ist weg!

newspaper die Zeitung

This is Dad's newspaper.
Das hier ist Vatis Zeitung.

next (beside) neben, (after that) danach, (next week) nächst-*

The yellow car is next to the red car.
Das gelbe Auto ist neben dem roten Auto.

next year
nächstes Jahr

nice (person) nett, (to look at) schön, (food) gut, lecker

Danny has made a nice picture.
Danny hat ein schönes Bild gemacht.

night die Nacht

It's night time. Es ist Nacht.

nod nicken

The dog is nodding.
Der Hund nickt.

noise das Geräusch, (loud) der Lärm

What's that noise?
Was ist das für ein Geräusch?

WAHH!

This baby is making a lot of noise.
Dieses Baby macht viel Lärm.

noisy laut

The boys are very noisy.
Die Jungen sind sehr laut.

a b c d e f g h i j k l m **n** o p q r s t u v w x y z
* You need to add an adjective ending to this word (see page 4).

Oo ocean *to* odd
o

nose — die Nase

Polly is pointing to Jack's nose.

Polly deutet auf Jacks Nase.

now — jetzt

The clown is holding a pie . . .
Der Clown hält eine Torte . . .

. . . now he falls down in it.
. . . jetzt fällt er hinein.

ocean — der Ozean

An ocean is a huge sea.

Ein Ozean ist ein riesiges Meer.

note — (message) die Notiz, (music) die Note

a note for Mom to see the dentist at 10:30
eine Notiz für Mutti

Zahnarzt 10.30 Uhr

number — (figure) die Zahl, (amount) die Anzahl, (street, phone) die Nummer

(981) 569-2636

Here's my phone number.
Hier ist meine Telefonnummer.

Two is an even number.
Zwei ist eine gerade Zahl.

o'clock — Uhr

one o'clock in the afternoon
ein Uhr nachmittags

seven o'clock in the morning
sieben Uhr morgens

notebook — das Notizbuch

This is Jack's notebook.
Das hier ist Jacks Notizbuch.

NOTIZEN

nurse — die Krankenschwester

The nurse is pushing Sally in a wheelchair.
Die Krankenschwester schiebt Sally mit dem Rollstuhl.

octopus — der Tintenfisch

An octopus has eight tentacles.

Ein Tintenfisch hat acht Fangarme.

notice — bemerken

The clown is hiding and Annie hasn't noticed him.
Der Clown hält sich versteckt und Annie hat ihn nicht bemerkt.

nut — die Nuss

Nuts are good to nibble.
Nüsse sind gut zum Knabbern.

odd — (number) ungerade, (strange) seltsam

The blue bunny is jumping on the odd numbers.
Das blaue Häschen springt auf die ungeraden Zahlen.

1   2   3   4   5

That's odd.   Das ist ja seltsam.

a b c d e f g h i j k l m **n o** p q r s t u v w x y z

often — oft

Mr. Dot and Jack often go and do the shopping.
Herr Dot und Jack gehen oft einkaufen.

onion — die Zwiebel

Onions have a strong taste.
Zwiebeln haben einen starken Geschmack.

opposite¹ — der Gegensatz

"Big" and "small" are opposites.
„Groß" und „klein" sind Gegensätze.

oil — das Öl

Sunflower oil is good for cooking.
Sonnenblumenöl ist gut zum Kochen.

only — nur, bloß

Becky only has two strawberries.
Becky hat nur zwei Erdbeeren *or* Becky hat bloß zwei Erdbeeren.

opposite² — gegenüber

Becky is sitting opposite her teddy bear.
Becky sitzt ihrem Teddy gegenüber.

old — alt

an old woman
eine alte Frau

an old shoe
ein alter Schuh

open¹ — auf/machen*, öffnen

Mr. Dot is opening the front door.
Herr Dot macht die Haustür auf.

Mrs. Dot is opening the box.
Frau Dot öffnet den Karton.

orange — (fruit) die Orange, (color) orangefarben

a juicy orange
eine saftige Orange

orange paint
orangefarbener Lack

once — einmal

They've been on a balloon trip once.
Sie haben einmal eine Ballonfahrt gemacht.

Once upon a time . . .
Es war einmal . . .

open² — offen, geöffnet

Mrs. Bird's store is open on Saturdays.
Frau Birds Geschäft ist samstags geöffnet.

Geöffnet: 9-17 Uhr

other — ander-**

Hast du noch andere Spielsachen?

Äh...nein.

Jenny's asking if Ethan has any other toys.

a b c d e f g h i j k l m n o p q r s t u v w x y z

* This is a separable verb (see page 99).
** You need to add an adjective ending to this word (see page 4).

outside   draußen, außen, außerhalb

Let's play outside!
Spielen wir draußen!

The monkey is outside the box.
Der Affe sitzt außerhalb der Kiste.

over   (above) über, (finished) zu Ende

The bird is flying over the tree.
Der Vogel fliegt über den Baum.

The party is over.
Die Party ist zu Ende.

owl   die Eule

Owls come out at night.
Eulen kommen nachts heraus.

own   eigen

Mrs. Bird has her own store.
Frau Bird hat ihr eigenes Geschäft.

page   die Seite

Polly is looking at page 72.

Polly sieht sich Seite 72 an.

paint¹   die Farbe, (on metal) der Lack

four bottles of paint
vier Flaschen Farbe

paint²   (picture) malen, (room) streichen

Shelley is painting a cat.
Shelley malt eine Katze.

I'm painting my bedroom blue.
Ich streiche mein Schlafzimmer blau.

pair   das Paar

a pair of striped socks
ein Paar gestreifte Socken

palace   der Palast, das Schloss

a palace with golden domes
ein Palast mit goldenen Kuppeln

pale   (face) blass, (color) hell, zart, blass

pale blue
hellblau

pale green
blassgrün

pale yellow
zartgelb

paper   das Papier, (newspaper) die Zeitung

some writing paper
etwas Schreibpapier

parachute   der Fallschirm

Mr. Brand is doing a parachute jump.
Herr Brand macht einen Fallschirmabsprung.

a b c d e f g h i j k l m o p q r s t u v w x y z

parents — die Eltern

Mr. and Mrs. Dot are Polly and Jack's parents.
Herr und Frau Dot sind Pollys und Jacks Eltern.

park¹ — der Park

Let's go and play in the park!
Gehen wir im Park spielen!

park² — parken

Jan parks in a parking lot.
Jan parkt auf einem Parkplatz.

PARKPLATZ
12 PLÄTZE

parrot — der Papagei

Some parrots can talk.
Manche Papageien können sprechen.

part — das Teil

A wheel is part of a car.
Ein Rad ist ein Autoteil.

party — die Party, die Feier

There are lots of guests at Ellie's party.
Es gibt viele Gäste auf Ellies Party.

pass — (give) reichen, (go past) vorbei/gehen*

They are passing the bank.
Sie gehen an der Bank vorbei.

Can you pass me the salt?
Kannst du mir das Salz reichen?

past¹ — die Vergangenheit

clothes from the past
Kleider aus der Vergangenheit

past² — an . . . vorbei

They run past the stores.
Sie laufen an den Geschäften vorbei.

path — der Weg, der Pfad

This path goes to the village.
Dieser Weg führt zum Dorf.

paw — die Pfote

This is the tiger's paw.
Das ist die Pfote des Tigers.

pay — zahlen, (for something) bezahlen

Who's paying?
Wer zahlt?

Ethan is paying for the apple.
Ethan bezahlt den Apfel.

a b c d e f g h i j k l m n o **p** q r s t u v w x y z

* This is a separable verb (see page 99).

pea — die Erbse	**pear** — die Birne	**penguin** — der Pinguin

pea — die Erbse

Peas are small, round vegetables.

Erbsen sind eine kleine, runde Gemüsesorte.

pear — die Birne

a sweet, juicy, green pear
eine süße, saftige, grüne Birne

penguin — der Pinguin

Penguins live in Antarctica.
Pinguine leben in der Antarktis.

peach — der Pfirsich

This peach is delicious.
Dieser Pfirsich ist lecker.

pebble — der Kieselstein

There are lots of pebbles on the beach.

Auf dem Strand sind viele Kieselsteine.

people — die Leute

These people are waiting for the start of the movie.

Diese Leute warten auf den Anfang des Films.

peak — (mountain) der Gipfel, (cap) der Schild, der Schirm

a snow-capped peak
ein schneebedeckter Gipfel

a cap with a peak
eine Schildmütze

pen — (ballpoint) der Kuli, der Kugelschreiber, (ink) der Füller

This is my new pen.

Das hier ist mein neuer Kugelschreiber.

pepper — (spice) der Pfeffer, (vegetable) die Paprikaschote

a pepper mill
eine Pfeffermühle

green, red and yellow peppers
grüne, rote und gelbe Paprikaschoten

peanut — die Erdnuss

a package of salted peanuts
eine Packung gesalzene Erdnüsse

pencil — der Bleistift

I'm drawing in pencil.
Ich zeichne mit Bleistift.

person — der Mensch, die Person

There is only one person here.
Es steht nur ein Mensch hier.

It costs two euros per person.
Es kostet zwei Euro pro Person.

a b c d e f g h i j k l m n o **p** q r s t u v w x y z

pet   das Haustier

some pets
ein paar
Haustiere

pick (choose) **aus/suchen*,**
(flowers, fruit) **pflücken**

Oliver has
picked an
apple and
a cupcake.

Oliver hat
einen Apfel
und einen
Kuchen
ausgesucht.

I'm picking some flowers.
Ich pflücke ein paar Blumen.

pillow   das Kopfkissen

a big, soft pillow
ein großes, weiches Kopfkissen

phone   das Telefon

a yellow phone
ein gelbes Telefon

picnic   das Picknick

Amy is having a picnic.
Amy macht
ein Picknick.

pilot   der Pilot
die Pilotin

Jim wants to
be a pilot.
Jim will
Pilot werden.

photo   das Foto

Polly is looking
at some
photos.

Polly sieht sich
ein paar Fotos an.

picture   das Bild

Shelley's painted a
very nice picture.
Shelley hat ein
sehr schönes
Bild gemalt.

pineapple   die Ananas

A pineapple is a
kind of tropical fruit.
Eine Ananas
ist eine
tropische
Obstsorte.

piano   das Klavier

I play the
piano.
Ich spiele
Klavier.

Polly has
a toy piano.
Polly hat ein
Spielzeugklavier.

piece   das Stück,
das Teil

a piece
of cake
ein
Stück
Kuchen

a jigsaw puzzle with nine pieces
ein Puzzle mit neun Teilen

pizza   die Pizza

a vegetarian pizza
eine vegetarische Pizza

a b c d e f g h i j k l m n o **p** q r s t u v w x y z

* This is a separable verb (see page 99).   58

place   die Stelle, der Ort, der Platz

Save me a place!
Halte mir einen Platz frei!

a good place to have lunch
ein guter Ort, um zu Mittag zu essen

plan¹   der Plan

a plan of the first floor

das Schlafzimmer
das Wohnzimmer
das Badezimmer

ein Plan des ersten Stocks

plan²   planen

Mrs. Dot is planning a party.
Frau Dot plant eine Party.

Datum: 22. Juni
Gäste:
Alex
Becky
Danny
Ellie

plane   das Flugzeug

The plane is landing.
Das Flugzeug landet.

planet   der Planet

a planet with rings
ein Planet mit Ringen

plant   die Pflanze

a potted plant
eine Topfpflanze

plate   der Teller

a clean plate
ein sauberer Teller

play   spielen

The children are playing outside.
Die Kinder spielen draußen.

Neil is playing soccer.
Neil spielt Fußball.

playground   (school) der Schulhof, (park) der Spielplatz

the playground in the park
der Spielplatz im Park

please   bitte

Becky is asking if she can please have some more strawberries.

Kann ich bitte noch Erdbeeren haben?

plum   die Pflaume

a nice, ripe plum
eine schöne, reife Pflaume

pocket   die Tasche

Renata is putting her hands in her pockets.
Renata steckt die Hände in die Taschen.

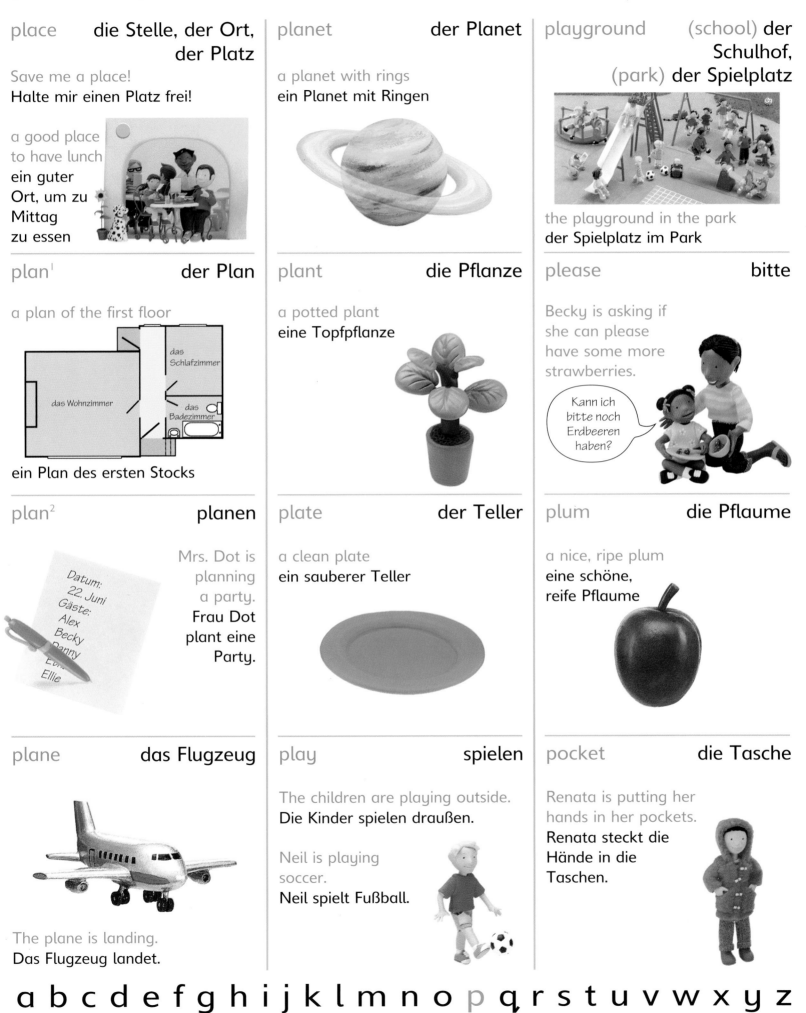

a b c d e f g h i j k l m n o p q r s t u v w x y z

poem — das Gedicht

Shelley has written a poem about her cat.
Shelley hat ein Gedicht über ihre Katze geschrieben.

Meine Katze
Meine Katze ist ganz weiß,
Ihr Schwanz ist lang
und ihr Fell ist weich.
Sie sitzt in der Sonne
und schnurrt und schläft,
Bis sie Hunger hat
und jagen geht.
Nachts kommt sie leise
in mein Bett,
Und wir schlafen
beide, bis Mutti
uns weckt.

point¹ — (sharp) die Spitze, (score) der Punkt

the pencil point
die Bleistiftspitze

We're playing a game, and I already have forty points.
Wir spielen ein Spiel und ich habe schon vierzig Punkte.

point² — deuten, zeigen

Polly is pointing to Jack's nose.
Polly deutet auf Jacks Nase.

Don't point!
Zeig nicht mit dem Finger!

police — die Polizei

Brian works for the police.
Brian arbeitet bei der Polizei.

police car — das Polizeiauto

There is no one in the police car.
Niemand ist im Polizeiauto.

pond — der Teich

a duck pond
ein Ententeich

pony — das Pony

a small pony
ein kleines Pony

pool — das Schwimmbad, das Schwimmbecken

There's a children's pool in the park.
Im Park ist ein Kinderschwimmbecken.

poor — arm

rich people and poor people
reiche Leute und arme Leute

Poor Ross! He has a tummy ache.
Der arme Ross! Er hat Bauchschmerzen.

potato — die Kartoffel

Potatoes grow underground.
Kartoffeln wachsen unter der Erde.

present — das Geschenk

a surprise present for Polly
ein Überraschungsgeschenk für Polly

press — drücken

Danny is pressing down the blue paper with his hands.
Danny drückt mit den Händen auf das blaue Papier.

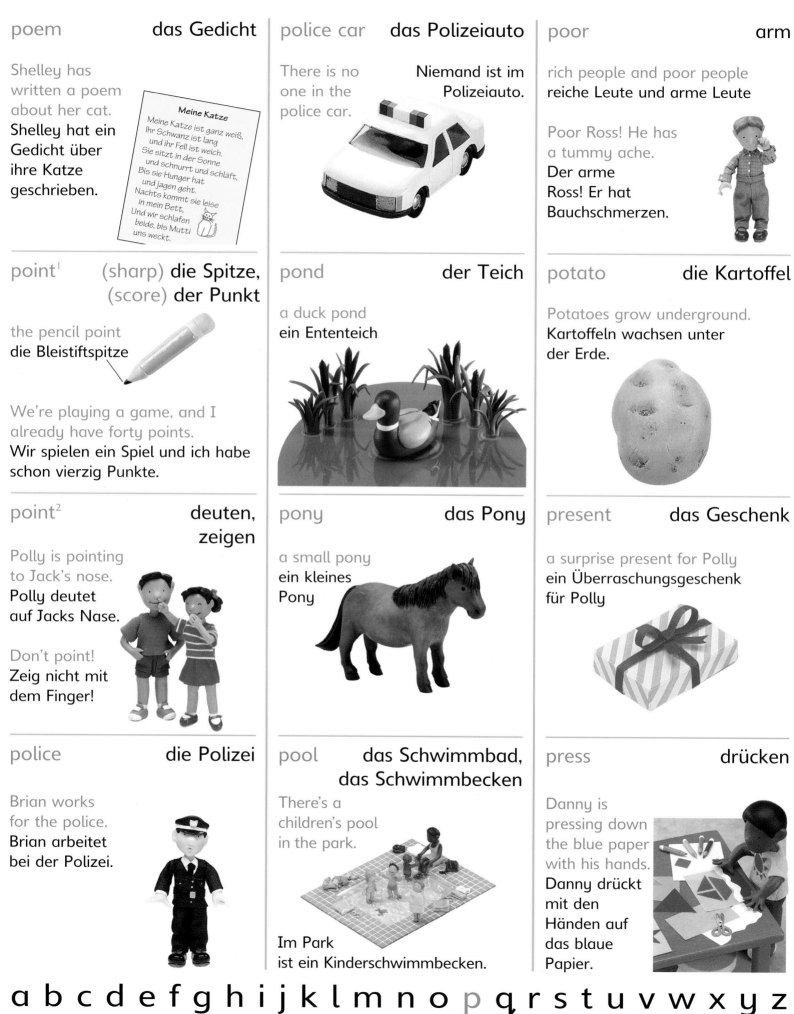

a b c d e f g h i j k l m n o p q r s t u v w x y z

pretend *to* puppet

pretend　　　　**tun als ob**

Nicholas is pretending to be asleep.

Nicholas tut, als ob er schläft.

pretty　　　　**hübsch**

Anya has a pretty red dress.
Anya hat ein hübsches rotes Kleid.

price　　　　**der Preis**

The watermelons are two for the price of one.

2 zum Preis von 1

prince　　　　**der Prinz**

a brave prince　　ein tapferer Prinz

princess　　　　**die Prinzessin**

a beautiful princess
eine schöne Prinzessin

prize　　　　**der Preis**

Neil's team has won a prize.
Neils Mannschaft hat einen Preis gewonnen.

promise　　　　**versprechen**

Ich nehme dich mit in den Park, ich verspreche es dir.

Minnie's dad is promising to take her to the park.

puddle　　　　**die Pfütze**

Alex is jumping in the puddles.
Alex hüpft in die Pfützen.

pull　　　　**ziehen**

Jack is pulling the package.

Thomas　　Jack

Jack zieht am Paket.

pumpkin　　　　**der Kürbis**

A pumpkin is a large fruit.
Ein Kürbis ist eine große Frucht.

pupil　　**der Schüler die Schülerin**

Mr. Levy and his pupils

Herr Levy und seine Schüler

puppet　　**die Puppe, (on strings) die Marionette**

This puppet is wearing funny clothes.
Diese Marionette hat komische Kleider an.

a b c d e f g h i j k l m n o **p** q r s t u v w x y z

61

puppy — das Hündchen

A puppy is a young dog.

Ein Hündchen ist ein junger Hund.

push — schieben

Thomas is pushing the package.

Thomas

Jack

Thomas schiebt das Paket.

put — (set down) stellen, setzen, legen, (put inside) stecken

Oliver is putting the bottle on the table.
Oliver stellt die Flasche auf den Tisch.

puzzle — (jigsaw) das Puzzle, (wordgame) das Rätsel

an easy puzzle — ein leichtes Puzzle

quack — quaken

Ducks quack.
Enten quaken.

Quak! Quak!

quarter — das Viertel

a quarter past three
Viertel nach drei

a quarter of the cake
ein Viertel des Kuchens

queen — die Königin

Joy is dressed up as a queen.
Joy ist als Königin verkleidet.

question — die Frage

Polly is asking a question: what's the clown called?

Wie heißt du?

Polly stellt eine Frage.

quick — schnell

Grace is very quick on her skateboard.

Grace fährt sehr schnell mit ihrem Skateboard.

quiet — leise, ruhig, still

Anna is very quiet – Milo doesn't hear her.
Anna ist sehr still – Milo hört sie nicht.

quite — (fairly) ziemlich, (completely) ganz

I'm quite tired.
Ich bin ziemlich müde.

Mr. Bun hasn't quite finished.
Herr Bun ist nicht ganz fertig.

quiz — das Quiz

This is a quiz about animals.
Das ist ein Quiz über Tiere.

Tierquiz
1) Welches ist das größte Tier der Welt?
2) Was für ein Tier ist der Tukan?
3) Wo in der Welt kann man Löwen und Elefanten sehen?

a b c d e f g h i j k l m n o p q r s t u v w x y z

Rr rabbit *to* real

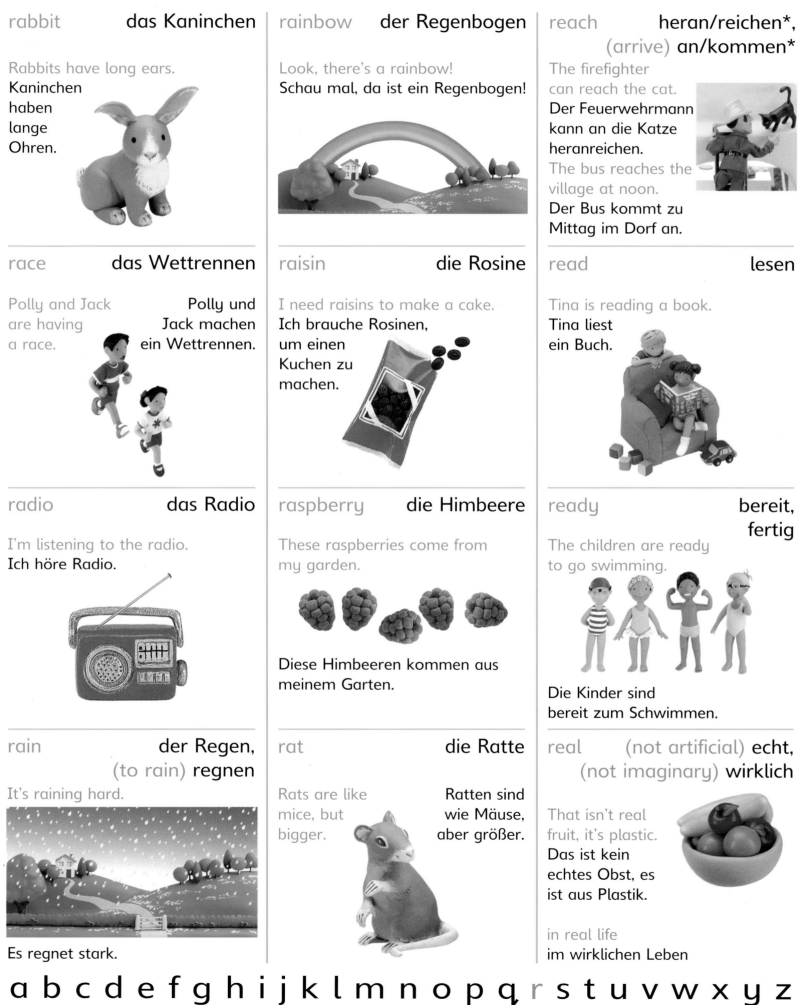

rabbit   das Kaninchen

Rabbits have long ears.
Kaninchen haben lange Ohren.

rainbow   der Regenbogen

Look, there's a rainbow!
Schau mal, da ist ein Regenbogen!

reach   heran/reichen*, (arrive) an/kommen*

The firefighter can reach the cat.
Der Feuerwehrmann kann an die Katze heranreichen.
The bus reaches the village at noon.
Der Bus kommt zu Mittag im Dorf an.

race   das Wettrennen

Polly and Jack are having a race.
Polly und Jack machen ein Wettrennen.

raisin   die Rosine

I need raisins to make a cake.
Ich brauche Rosinen, um einen Kuchen zu machen.

read   lesen

Tina is reading a book.
Tina liest ein Buch.

radio   das Radio

I'm listening to the radio.
Ich höre Radio.

raspberry   die Himbeere

These raspberries come from my garden.
Diese Himbeeren kommen aus meinem Garten.

ready   bereit, fertig

The children are ready to go swimming.
Die Kinder sind bereit zum Schwimmen.

rain   der Regen, (to rain) regnen

It's raining hard.
Es regnet stark.

rat   die Ratte

Rats are like mice, but bigger.
Ratten sind wie Mäuse, aber größer.

real   (not artificial) echt, (not imaginary) wirklich

That isn't real fruit, it's plastic.
Das ist kein echtes Obst, es ist aus Plastik.

in real life
im wirklichen Leben

a b c d e f g h i j k l m n o p q **r** s t u v w x y z

* This is a separable verb (see page 99).

recorder   **die Blockflöte**

At school I'm learning to play the recorder.
In der Schule lerne ich, Blockflöte zu spielen.

refrigerator **der Kühlschrank**

The refrigerator is full.
Der Kühlschrank ist voll.

remember **sich erinnern an**

Fiona can remember the date of her friend's birthday.
Fiona kann sich an den Geburtstag ihrer Freundin erinnern.

Du hast am 26. Mai Geburtstag.

reply   **antworten**

Willst du in den Park gehen?

Ja, bitte.

Minnie is replying to her dad.
Minnie antwortet ihrem Vati.

rescue   **retten**

Mr. Sparks has rescued the cat.
Herr Sparks hat die Katze gerettet.

rhinoceros **das Nashorn** *or* rhino

Rhinos live in hot countries.
Nashörner leben in heißen Ländern.

ribbon   **das Band**

Becky has green ribbons in her hair.
Becky hat grüne Bänder im Haar.

rice   **der Reis**

I prefer rice to pasta.
Ich esse lieber Reis als Nudeln.

rich   **reich**

Natalie is a very rich singer.
Natalie ist eine sehr reiche Sängerin.

ride   (horse) **reiten**, (bicycle) **fahren**

Martin is riding his horse.
Martin reitet auf seinem Pferd.

I like riding my bike.
Ich fahre gern Rad.

right   (not wrong) **richtig**, (not left) **rechts, recht-***

That's the right answer.
Das ist die richtige Antwort.

Greta has the puppet on her right hand.
Greta hat die Puppe an der rechten Hand.

ring¹   **der Ring**

a ring with a red stone
ein Ring mit einem roten Stein

the rings of Saturn
die Saturnringe

a b c d e f g h i j k l m n o p q r s t u v w x y z

* You need to add an adjective ending to this word (see page 4).

ring² klingeln, läuten

The phone's ringing.
Das Telefon klingelt.

Klingeling!

robot der Roboter

a toy robot
ein Spielzeugroboter

room (space) der Platz, (in house) das Zimmer

On this plan, there are six rooms.
Auf diesem Plan sind sechs Zimmer.

Is there room for me?
Ist hier Platz für mich?

ripe reif

The melon, the avocado and the watermelon are all ripe.

Die Melone, die Avocado und die Wassermelone sind alle reif.

rock (stone) der Fels, der Stein, (music) die Rockmusik

There are rocks on the beach.
Am Strand sind Felsen.
Steve likes playing rock music.
Steve spielt gern Rockmusik.

rope das Seil

The rope is neatly tied.
Das Seil ist ordentlich gebunden.

river der Fluss

The houses are by the river.

Die Häuser sind am Fluss.

rocket die Rakete

a toy rocket
eine Spielzeugrakete

rose die Rose

a red rose
eine rote Rose

road die Straße

The road goes into town.
Die Straße führt in die Stadt.

roof das Dach

This building has a blue roof.
Dieses Gebäude hat ein blaues Dach.

round rund

Most drums are round.

Die meisten Trommeln sind rund.

a b c d e f g h i j k l m n o p q **r** s t u v w x y z

rug (big) **der Teppich,** (small) **der Vorleger**

a soft rug
ein weicher Teppich

ruler **das Lineal**

You can use a ruler to draw straight lines.
Mit einem Lineal kann man gerade Linien zeichnen.

run **laufen, rennen**

Polly and Jack are running.
Polly und Jack laufen *or* Polly und Jack rennen.

rush (move quickly) **eilen, laufen,** (hurry) **sich beeilen**

They are rushing after Pip.
Sie eilen Pip hinterher.

sad **traurig**

Liddy is sad without her mommy.
Liddy ist traurig ohne ihre Mutti.

saddle **der Sattel**

Martin's horse has a new saddle.
Martins Pferd hat einen neuen Sattel.

safe **sicher**

a safe place to cross the street
eine sichere Stelle, um die Straße zu überqueren

sailor **der Matrose die Matrosin**

Gareth is dressed up as a sailor.
Gareth ist als Matrose verkleidet.

salad **der Salat**

a mixed salad
ein gemischter Salat

salami **die Salami**

This is Italian salami.
Das hier ist italienische Salami.

salt **das Salz**

I've spilled the salt.
Ich habe das Salz verschüttet.

same **gleich, (der-, die-,) dasselbe***

The twins always wear the same colors.
Die Zwillinge tragen immer die gleichen Farben.

a b c d e f g h i j k l m n o p q r s t u v w x y z

* You use *derselbe* with masculine words, *dieselbe* with feminine words, *dasselbe* with neuter words and *dieselben* with plural words: We go to the same school. Wir gehen auf dieselbe Schule.

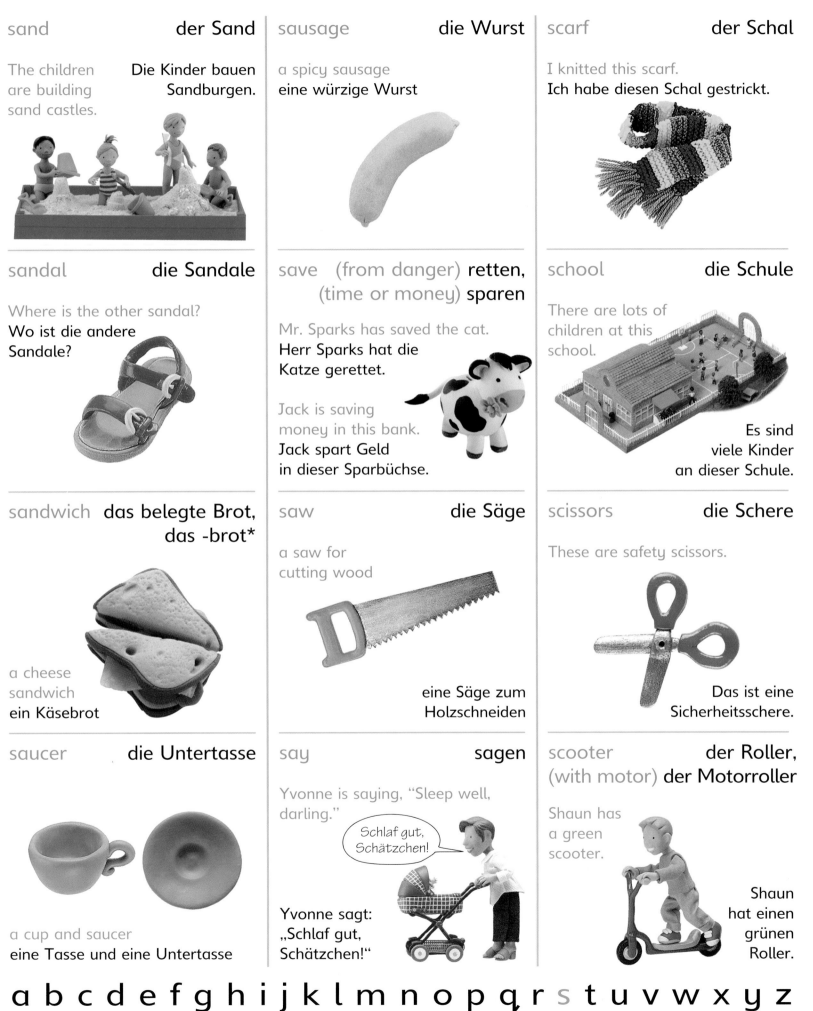

sand   der Sand

The children are building sand castles.

Die Kinder bauen Sandburgen.

sandal   die Sandale

Where is the other sandal?
Wo ist die andere Sandale?

sandwich   das belegte Brot, das -brot*

a cheese sandwich
ein Käsebrot

saucer   die Untertasse

a cup and saucer
eine Tasse und eine Untertasse

sausage   die Wurst

a spicy sausage
eine würzige Wurst

save   (from danger) retten, (time or money) sparen

Mr. Sparks has saved the cat.
Herr Sparks hat die Katze gerettet.

Jack is saving money in this bank.
Jack spart Geld in dieser Sparbüchse.

saw   die Säge

a saw for cutting wood

eine Säge zum Holzschneiden

say   sagen

Yvonne is saying, "Sleep well, darling."

Schlaf gut, Schätzchen!

Yvonne sagt: „Schlaf gut, Schätzchen!"

scarf   der Schal

I knitted this scarf.
Ich habe diesen Schal gestrickt.

school   die Schule

There are lots of children at this school.

Es sind viele Kinder an dieser Schule.

scissors   die Schere

These are safety scissors.

Das ist eine Sicherheitsschere.

scooter   der Roller, (with motor) der Motorroller

Shaun has a green scooter.

Shaun hat einen grünen Roller.

a b c d e f g h i j k l m n o p q r **s** t u v w x y z

* You need to add the type of sandwich onto the front of this word: a ham sandwich – ein Schinkenbrot.

sea — das Meer, die See

The sea is calm today.
Das Meer ist heute ruhig.

seal — der Seehund

Seals live by the sea.
Seehunde leben am Meer.

search — suchen

They are searching for their friend.
Sie suchen nach ihrem Freund.

seat — (chair) der Sitz, (place to sit) der Platz

There are three seats free.
Drei Plätze sind frei.

secret — das Geheimnis

Amy is telling Anna a secret.
Amy vertraut Anna ein Geheimnis an.

see — sehen, (visit) besuchen

Annie can't see the clown.
Annie sieht den Clown nicht.

I'm going to see my grandparents.
Ich gehe meine Großeltern besuchen.

sell — verkaufen

Mrs. Hussain is selling Ethan an apple.
Frau Hussain verkauft Ethan einen Apfel.

send — schicken

Jack is sending a letter to his friend.
Jack schickt seinem Freund einen Brief.

sentence — der Satz

This is a complete sentence.
My dad plays tennis.
Mein Vati spielt Tennis.
Das ist ein ganzer Satz.

sew — nähen

Robert is sewing his shirt.
Robert näht sein Hemd.

shadow — der Schatten

Look at Robert's shadow!
Schau mal Roberts Schatten an!

shake — schütteln

Anton likes shaking his rattle.
Anton schüttelt gern seine Rassel.

a b c d e f g h i j k l m n o p q r s t u v w x y z

shallow — **seicht, nicht tief**

The children's pool is shallow.

Das Kinderschwimmbecken ist nicht tief.

sharp — **(edge) scharf, (point) spitz**

Watch out! The knife is sharp.
Pass auf! Das Messer ist scharf.

This is a sharp pencil.
Das ist ein spitzer Bleistift.

shell — **(sea) die Muschel, (eggs, nuts) die Schale**

I collect shells.

Ich sammle Muscheln.

an eggshell
eine Eierschale

shampoo — **das Shampoo**

Can you lend me some shampoo?

Kannst du mir etwas Shampoo leihen?

sheep — **das Schaf**

Wool comes from sheep.
Schafe geben Wolle.

ship — **das Schiff**

a cruise ship
ein Kreuzfahrtschiff

share — **teilen**

Bill is sharing his cherries with Ben.
Bill teilt seine Kirschen mit Ben.

sheet — **(of paper) das Blatt, (on bed) das Bettlaken**

a white sheet
ein weißes Bettlaken

a sheet of writing paper
ein Blatt Schreibpapier

shirt — **das Hemd**

Milo is wearing a plaid shirt.
Milo hat ein kariertes Hemd an.

shark — **der Hai**

This shark lives in tropical seas.

shelf — **das Regal**

Sam keeps his things on this shelf.
Sam bewahrt seine Sachen auf diesem Regal auf.

shoe — **der Schuh**

These are Robert's new shoes.

Dieser Hai lebt in tropischen Meeren.

Das sind Roberts neue Schuhe.

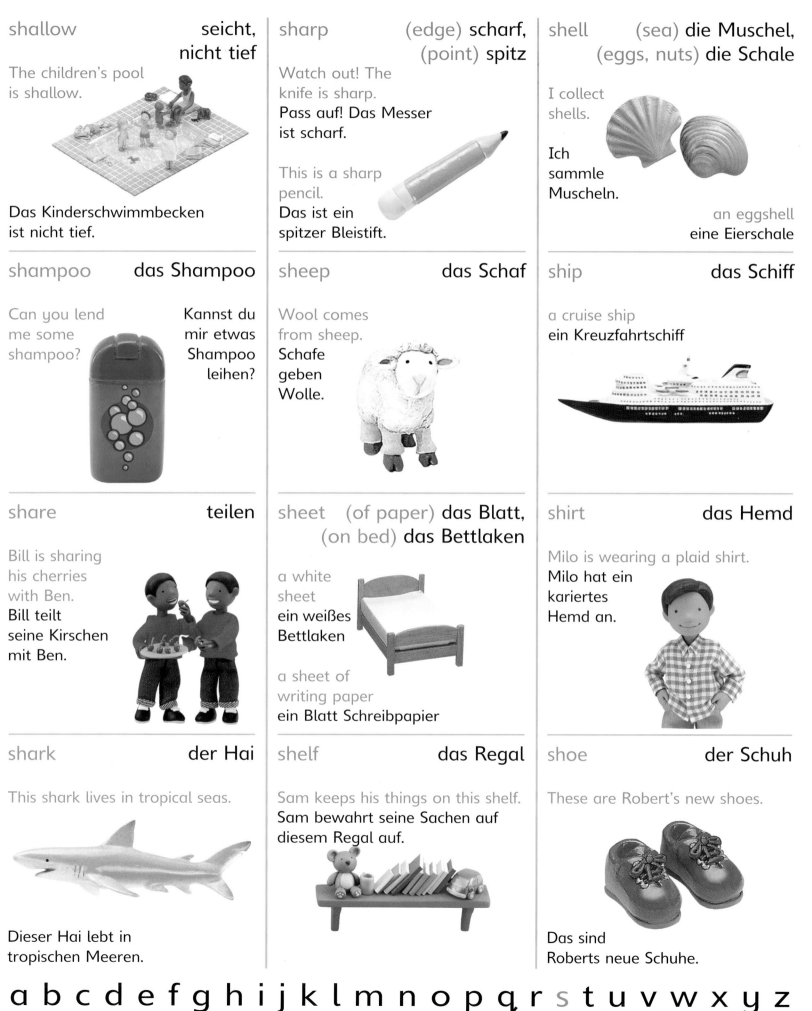

a b c d e f g h i j k l m n o p q r s t u v w x y z

short   **kurz**

Maisie has short hair.
Maisie hat kurze Haare.

shorts   **die Shorts, die kurze Hose**

brightly colored shorts
bunte Shorts *or* **eine bunte kurze Hose**

shoulder   **die Schulter**

This is Jack's shoulder.
Das hier ist Jacks Schulter.—

shout   **rufen, (very loudly) schreien**

HALT, PIP!

Jack is shouting, "Stop, Pip!"
Jack ruft: „Halt, Pip!"

show   **zeigen**

Jack is showing Thomas his hands.
Jack zeigt Thomas die Hände.

Show me your picture.
Zeig mir dein Bild!

shower   **(rain) der Schauer, (for washing) die Dusche**

Robert is in the shower.
Robert steht unter der Dusche.

sun and showers
Sonne und Schauer

shrink   **kleiner werden, (clothes) ein/laufen***

Wool clothes sometimes shrink in hot water.
Wollkleider laufen manchmal im heißen Wasser ein.

shut   **zu/machen*, schließen**

Danny is shutting the door.
Danny macht die Tür zu *or* **Danny schließt die Tür.**

side   **die Seite**

I'm on your side.
Ich bin auf deiner Seite.

I write on both sides of the paper.
Ich schreibe auf beide Seiten des Papiers.

sign¹   **(road) das Schild, (symbol) das Zeichen**

This sign means "no buses."
Dieses Schild bedeutet „keine Busse".

@ is the sign for "at."
@ ist das Zeichen für „bei".

sign²   **unterschreiben**

The paper says "Sign here please."

Bitte hier unterschreiben

since   **seit**

They've been waiting since noon.
Sie warten schon seit Mittag.

a b c d e f g h i j k l m n o p q r **s** t u v w x y z

sing *to* sleeve

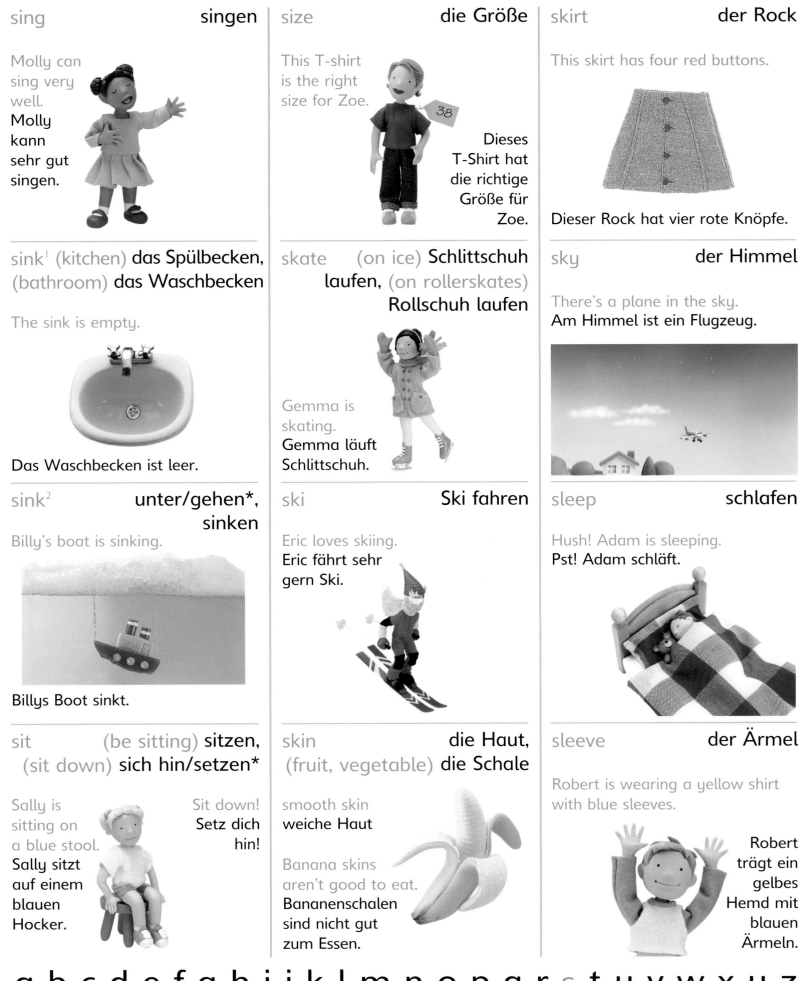

sing — **singen**

Molly can sing very well.
Molly kann sehr gut singen.

sink¹ (kitchen) **das Spülbecken,** (bathroom) **das Waschbecken**

The sink is empty.

Das Waschbecken ist leer.

sink² — **unter/gehen*, sinken**

Billy's boat is sinking.

Billys Boot sinkt.

sit (be sitting) **sitzen,** (sit down) **sich hin/setzen***

Sally is sitting on a blue stool.
Sally sitzt auf einem blauen Hocker.

Sit down!
Setz dich hin!

size — **die Größe**

This T-shirt is the right size for Zoe.

Dieses T-Shirt hat die richtige Größe für Zoe.

skate (on ice) **Schlittschuh laufen,** (on rollerskates) **Rollschuh laufen**

Gemma is skating.
Gemma läuft Schlittschuh.

ski — **Ski fahren**

Eric loves skiing.
Eric fährt sehr gern Ski.

skin — **die Haut,** (fruit, vegetable) **die Schale**

smooth skin
weiche Haut

Banana skins aren't good to eat.
Bananenschalen sind nicht gut zum Essen.

skirt — **der Rock**

This skirt has four red buttons.

Dieser Rock hat vier rote Knöpfe.

sky — **der Himmel**

There's a plane in the sky.
Am Himmel ist ein Flugzeug.

sleep — **schlafen**

Hush! Adam is sleeping.
Pst! Adam schläft.

sleeve — **der Ärmel**

Robert is wearing a yellow shirt with blue sleeves.

Robert trägt ein gelbes Hemd mit blauen Ärmeln.

a b c d e f g h i j k l m n o p q r s t u v w x y z

* This is a separable verb (see page 99).

slice   die Scheibe, (cake) das Stück

a slice of bread
eine Scheibe Brot

a slice of cake
ein Stück Kuchen

slide¹   die Rutschbahn

There's a slide in the park.
Im Park ist eine Rutschbahn.

slide²   rutschen

Denise is sliding down first.
Denise rutscht zuerst hinunter.

slip   aus/rutschen*

Anna has slipped on the banana skin.
Anna ist auf der Bananenschale ausgerutscht.

slipper   der Hausschuh

Polly has pink, bunny-shaped slippers.
Polly hat rosa, häschenförmige Hausschuhe.

slow   langsam

This is an old, slow train.
Das hier ist ein alter, langsamer Zug.

slowly   langsam

Sally is going slowly.
Sally fährt langsam.

slug   die Nacktschnecke

There are lots of slugs in the garden.
Im Garten sind viele Nacktschnecken.

small   klein

Leila is a small girl.
Leila ist ein kleines Mädchen.

smell   riechen

Smell the flowers!
Riech mal die Blumen!

This cat smells bad.
Diese Katze riecht schlecht.

smile   lächeln

Jack is smiling.
Jack lächelt.

smooth   glatt, (skin) weich

Babies have smooth skin.
Babys haben weiche Haut.

The road is smooth here.
Hier ist die Straße glatt.

a b c d e f g h i j k l m n o p q r **s** t u v w x y z

snail — die Schnecke

A snail has a shell on its back.

Eine Schnecke hat ein Haus auf ihrem Rücken.

snake — die Schlange

There's a snake in the tree.
Auf dem Baum ist eine Schlange.

snow — der Schnee, (to snow) schneien

They're playing in the snow.
Sie spielen im Schnee.

soap — die Seife

My soap is pink.
Meine Seife ist rosa.

soccer — der Fußball

Neil plays soccer every Saturday.
Neil spielt jeden Samstag Fußball.

sock — die Socke

Luke has striped socks.
Luke hat gestreifte Socken.

sofa — das Sofa

a comfortable sofa
ein bequemes Sofa

soft — weich

The kitten has soft, white fur.

Das Kätzchen hat ein weiches, weißes Fell.

soil — die Erde

My plant needs good soil.
Meine Pflanze braucht gute Erde.

soldier — der Soldat

Tony is dressed up as a soldier.
Tony ist als Soldat verkleidet.

song — das Lied

La la la la

Natalie is singing a song.
Natalie singt ein Lied.

soon — bald

It will soon be two o'clock.

Es ist bald zwei Uhr.

a b c d e f g h i j k l m n o p q r s t u v w x y z

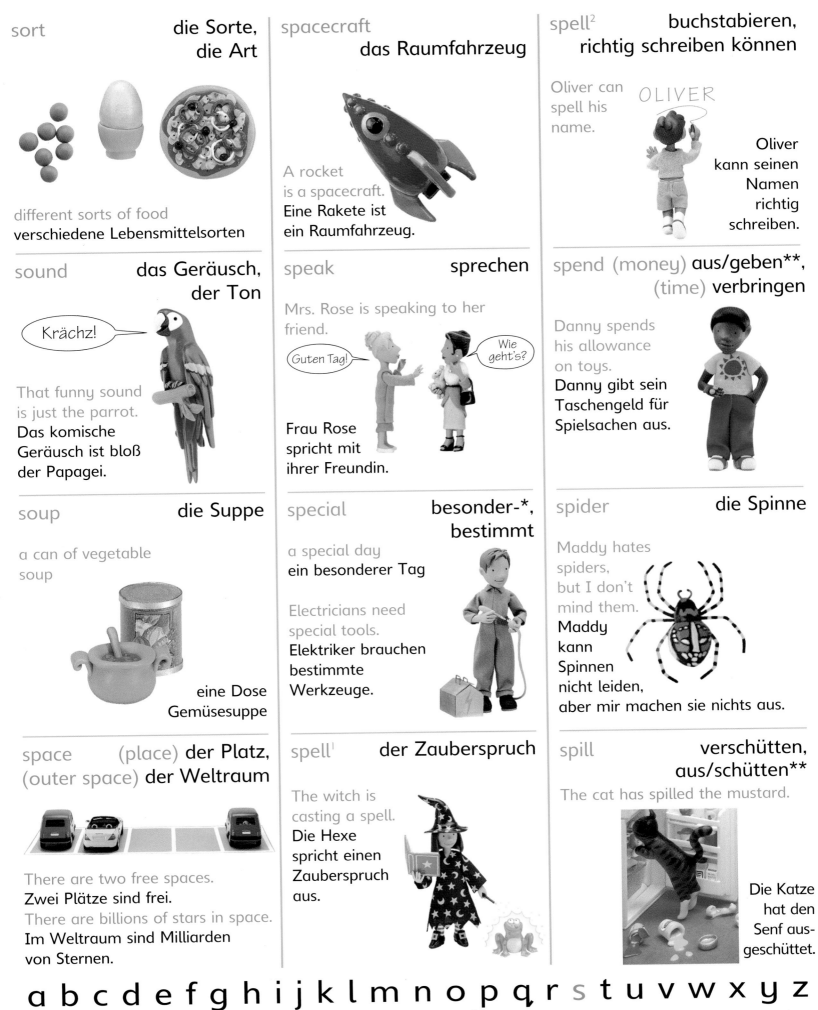

sort — die Sorte, die Art

different sorts of food
verschiedene Lebensmittelsorten

sound — das Geräusch, der Ton

Krächz!

That funny sound is just the parrot.
Das komische Geräusch ist bloß der Papagei.

soup — die Suppe

a can of vegetable soup

eine Dose Gemüsesuppe

space — (place) der Platz, (outer space) der Weltraum

There are two free spaces.
Zwei Plätze sind frei.
There are billions of stars in space.
Im Weltraum sind Milliarden von Sternen.

spacecraft — das Raumfahrzeug

A rocket is a spacecraft.
Eine Rakete ist ein Raumfahrzeug.

speak — sprechen

Mrs. Rose is speaking to her friend.

Guten Tag!

Wie geht's?

Frau Rose spricht mit ihrer Freundin.

special — besonder-*, bestimmt

a special day
ein besonderer Tag

Electricians need special tools.
Elektriker brauchen bestimmte Werkzeuge.

spell¹ — der Zauberspruch

The witch is casting a spell.
Die Hexe spricht einen Zauberspruch aus.

spell² — buchstabieren, richtig schreiben können

Oliver can spell his name.

OLIVER

Oliver kann seinen Namen richtig schreiben.

spend — (money) aus/geben**, (time) verbringen

Danny spends his allowance on toys.
Danny gibt sein Taschengeld für Spielsachen aus.

spider — die Spinne

Maddy hates spiders, but I don't mind them.
Maddy kann Spinnen nicht leiden, aber mir machen sie nichts aus.

spill — verschütten, aus/schütten**

The cat has spilled the mustard.

Die Katze hat den Senf ausgeschüttet.

a b c d e f g h i j k l m n o p q r **s** t u v w x y z

* You need to add an adjective ending to this word (see page 4).
** This is a separable verb (see page 99).

spinach	der Spinat

Spinach is a leafy vegetable.

Spinat ist ein Blattgemüse.

splash	spritzen, verspritzen

Polly is splashing water everywhere.

Polly spritzt überall Wasser hin.

sponge	der Schwamm

a bath sponge
ein Badeschwamm

spoon	der Löffel

I need a spoon to eat my soup.

Ich brauche einen Löffel, um meine Suppe zu essen.

sport	der Sport

They all enjoy playing sports.

Sie treiben alle gern Sport.

spot[1]	der Fleck, der Punkt

This dog has black spots.
Dieser Hund hat schwarze Flecken.

a red skirt with yellow spots
ein roter Rock mit gelben Punkten

spot[2]	entdecken

I've spotted a clown.
Ich habe einen Clown entdeckt.

squirrel	das Eichhörnchen

a gray squirrel

ein graues Eichhörnchen

stairs	die Treppe

The stairs lead up to the first floor.
Die Treppe führt zum ersten Stock hinauf.

stamp	die Briefmarke

This letter has a stamp on it.
Auf diesem Brief ist eine Briefmarke.

Oliver Esser
Wurststraße 34
54321 Schokostadt

stand	(be standing) stehen, (stand up) auf/stehen*

Alex is standing.
Alex steht.

Stand up, please!
Steh bitte auf!

star	(in sky) der Stern, (person) der Star

The stars are twinkling.
Die Sterne funkeln.

Natalie, the singer, is a big star.
Natalie, die Sängerin, ist ein großer Star.

a b c d e f g h i j k l m n o p q r **s** t u v w x y z

* This is a separable verb (see page 99).

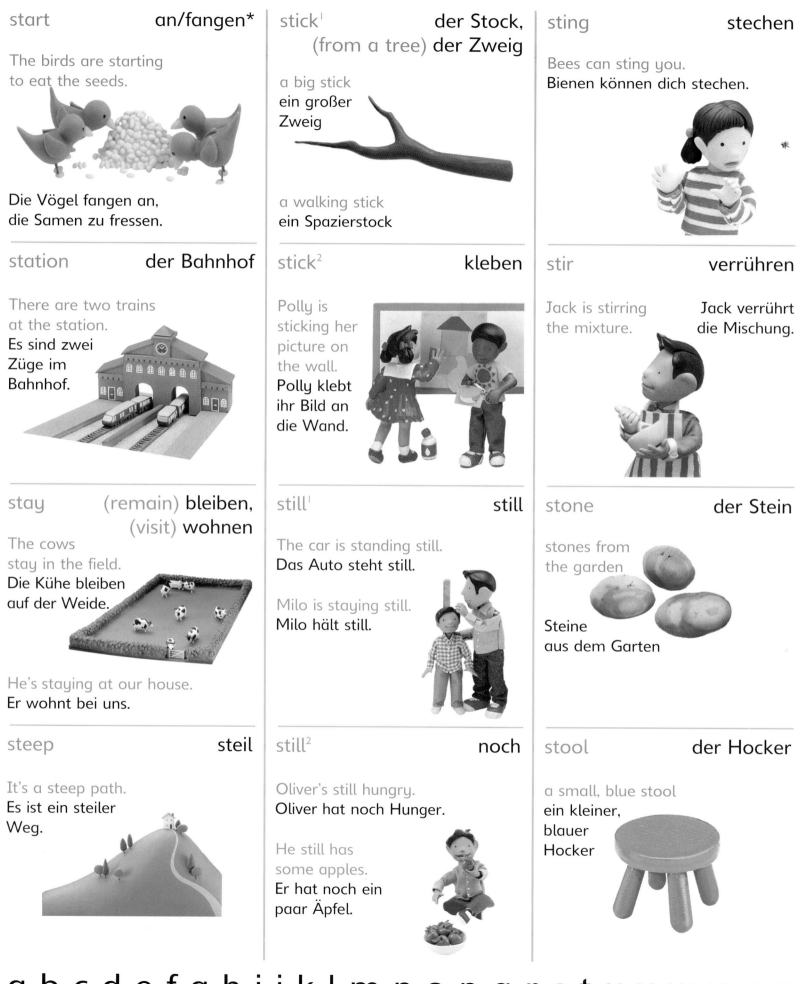

start an/fangen*

The birds are starting
to eat the seeds.

Die Vögel fangen an,
die Samen zu fressen.

station der Bahnhof

There are two trains
at the station.
Es sind zwei
Züge im
Bahnhof.

stay (remain) bleiben,
(visit) wohnen

The cows
stay in the field.
Die Kühe bleiben
auf der Weide.

He's staying at our house.
Er wohnt bei uns.

steep steil

It's a steep path.
Es ist ein steiler
Weg.

stick¹ der Stock,
(from a tree) der Zweig

a big stick
ein großer
Zweig

a walking stick
ein Spazierstock

stick² kleben

Polly is
sticking her
picture on
the wall.
Polly klebt
ihr Bild an
die Wand.

still¹ still

The car is standing still.
Das Auto steht still.

Milo is staying still.
Milo hält still.

still² noch

Oliver's still hungry.
Oliver hat noch Hunger.

He still has
some apples.
Er hat noch ein
paar Äpfel.

sting stechen

Bees can sting you.
Bienen können dich stechen.

stir verrühren

Jack is stirring Jack verrührt
the mixture. die Mischung.

stone der Stein

stones from
the garden

Steine
aus dem Garten

stool der Hocker

a small, blue stool
ein kleiner,
blauer
Hocker

a b c d e f g h i j k l m n o p q r s t u v w x y z

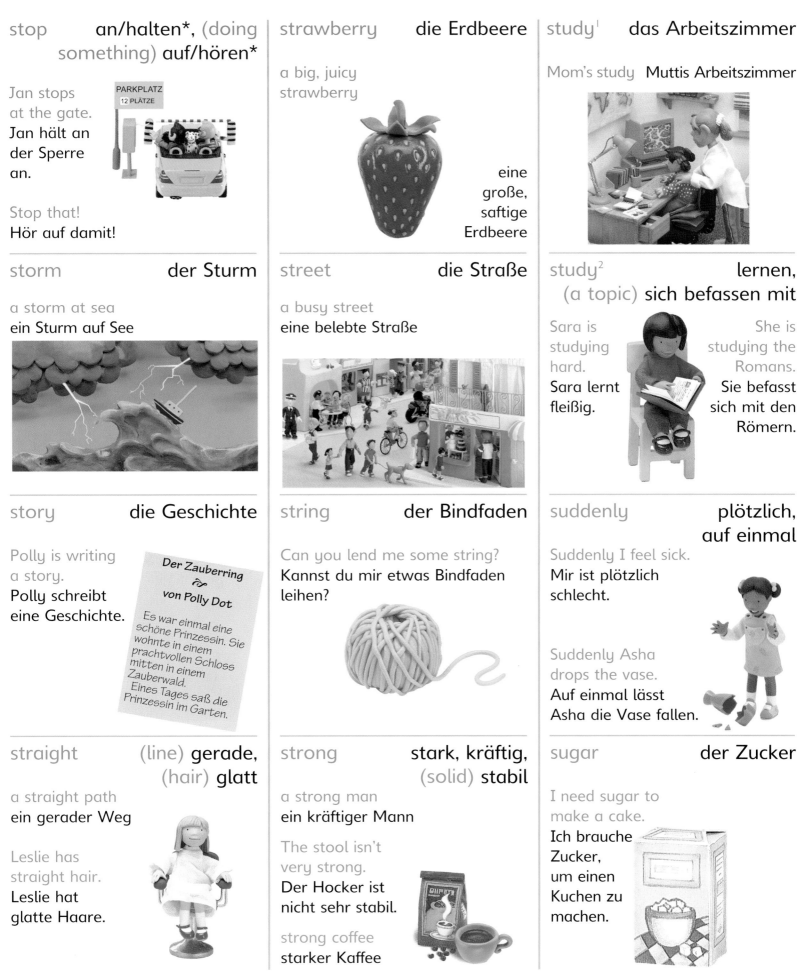

stop an/halten*, (doing something) auf/hören*

Jan stops at the gate.
Jan hält an der Sperre an.

PARKPLATZ 12 PLÄTZE

Stop that!
Hör auf damit!

storm der Sturm

a storm at sea
ein Sturm auf See

story die Geschichte

Polly is writing a story.
Polly schreibt eine Geschichte.

Der Zauberring
von Polly Dot

Es war einmal eine schöne Prinzessin. Sie wohnte in einem prachtvollen Schloss mitten in einem Zauberwald. Eines Tages saß die Prinzessin im Garten.

straight (line) gerade, (hair) glatt

a straight path
ein gerader Weg

Leslie has straight hair.
Leslie hat glatte Haare.

strawberry die Erdbeere

a big, juicy strawberry

eine große, saftige Erdbeere

street die Straße

a busy street
eine belebte Straße

string der Bindfaden

Can you lend me some string?
Kannst du mir etwas Bindfaden leihen?

strong stark, kräftig, (solid) stabil

a strong man
ein kräftiger Mann

The stool isn't very strong.
Der Hocker ist nicht sehr stabil.

strong coffee
starker Kaffee

study¹ das Arbeitszimmer

Mom's study Muttis Arbeitszimmer

study² lernen, (a topic) sich befassen mit

Sara is studying hard.
Sara lernt fleißig.

She is studying the Romans.
Sie befasst sich mit den Römern.

suddenly plötzlich, auf einmal

Suddenly I feel sick.
Mir ist plötzlich schlecht.

Suddenly Asha drops the vase.
Auf einmal lässt Asha die Vase fallen.

sugar der Zucker

I need sugar to make a cake.
Ich brauche Zucker, um einen Kuchen zu machen.

a b c d e f g h i j k l m n o p q r s t u v w x y z

* This is a separable verb (see page 99).

suitcase — **der Koffer**

This is Mr. Brand's suitcase.
Das ist Herr Brands Koffer.

sunglasses — **die Sonnenbrille**

Polly has pink sunglasses with blue flowers.

Polly hat eine rosa Sonnenbrille mit blauen Blumen darauf.

swan — **der Schwan**

There's a swan on the river.

Auf dem Fluss ist ein Schwan.

sum — **die Rechenaufgabe, die Summe**

These sums are easy.
Diese Rechenaufgaben sind leicht.

$$8 + 2 =$$
$$4 - 2 =$$
$$10 \times 4 =$$

supermarket — **der Supermarkt**

Dad is at the supermarket.
Vati ist im Supermarkt.

sweep — **fegen, kehren**

Anna is sweeping the path.
Anna fegt den Weg.

Shall I sweep the floor?
Soll ich kehren?

sun — **die Sonne**

The sun is shining.
Die Sonne scheint.

sure — **sicher**

Dad says, "Have we got everything? Are you sure?"
Vati sagt: „Haben wir alles? Bist du sicher?"

sweet — **(taste) süß, (cute) niedlich, süß**

That's a very sweet kitten.
Das ist ein sehr niedliches Kätzchen.

The cake is very sweet.
Der Kuchen ist sehr süß.

sunflower — **die Sonnenblume**

Aggie has some lovely sunflowers.

Aggie hat ein paar schöne Sonnenblumen.

surprise — **die Überraschung**

What a surprise!
Was für eine Überraschung!

BUH!

swim — **schwimmen**

Pete can swim very well.
Pete kann sehr gut schwimmen.

a b c d e f g h i j k l m n o p q r **s** t u v w x y z

Tt

t

swimming pool
das Schwimmbad

We're going to the swimming pool today.

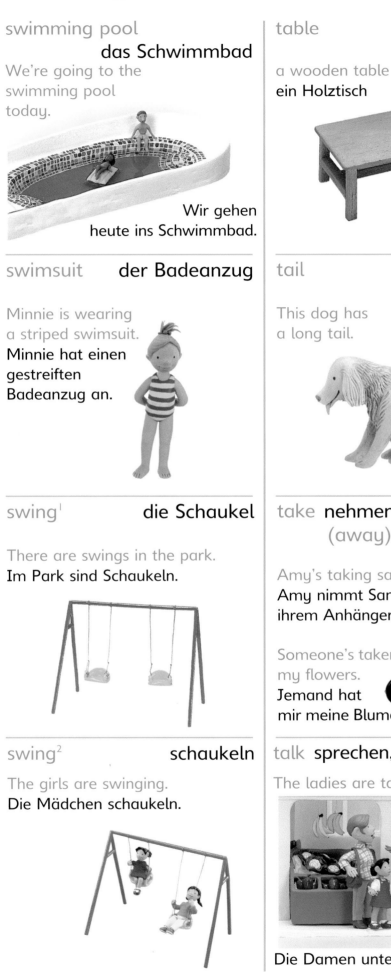

Wir gehen heute ins Schwimmbad.

swimsuit   der Badeanzug

Minnie is wearing a striped swimsuit.
Minnie hat einen gestreiften Badeanzug an.

swing¹   die Schaukel

There are swings in the park.
Im Park sind Schaukeln.

swing²   schaukeln

The girls are swinging.
Die Mädchen schaukeln.

table   der Tisch

a wooden table
ein Holztisch

tail   der Schwanz

This dog has a long tail.
Dieser Hund hat einen langen Schwanz.

take nehmen, mit/nehmen*, (away) weg/nehmen*

Amy's taking sand in her wagon.
Amy nimmt Sand in ihrem Anhänger mit.

Someone's taken my flowers.
Jemand hat mir meine Blumen weggenommen.

talk sprechen, sich unterhalten

The ladies are talking.

Die Damen unterhalten sich.

tall   (person, animal) groß, (building) hoch, hoh-**

A giraffe is a very tall animal.
Eine Giraffe ist ein sehr großes Tier.

a tall skyscraper
ein hoher Wolkenkratzer

taste   schmecken, (take a little) probieren

Ethan is tasting his ice cream.
Ethan probiert sein Eis.

It tastes good.
Es schmeckt gut.

taxi   das Taxi

a yellow taxi
ein gelbes Taxi

tea   der Tee

a tea bag
ein Teebeutel

a b c d e f g h i j k l m n o p q r s t u v w x y z

* This is a separable verb (see page 99).
** You need to add an adjective ending to this word (see page 4).

teacher · der Lehrer, die Lehrerin

Our teacher is Mr. Levy.

Unser Lehrer heißt Herr Levy.

team · die Mannschaft

This is Neil's team.

Das hier ist Neils Mannschaft.

teddy bear · der Teddy

This teddy bear has a red scarf.

Dieser Teddy hat einen roten Schal.

telephone · das Telefon

Where is the telephone, please?

Wo ist das Telefon, bitte?

television · das Fernsehen, (television set) der Fernseher

There's nothing on television this evening.

Heute Abend kommt nichts im Fernsehen.

a new television

ein neuer Fernseher

tell · sagen, (a story) erzählen

Mrs. Beef is telling them the story.

Frau Beef erzählt ihnen die Geschichte.

Tell me what you think.

Sag mir, was du meinst.

tent · das Zelt

Jack has a little, yellow tent.

Jack hat ein kleines, gelbes Zelt.

thank · danken, sich bedanken

Polly is thanking Marco for her present.

Polly dankt Marco für ihr Geschenk *or* Polly bedankt sich bei Marco für ihr Geschenk.

thin · dünn

thin string

dünner Bindfaden

a thin cat

eine dünne Katze

thing · die Sache, das Ding

Tina still has some things to do.

Tina hat noch einige Sachen zu erledigen.

What's that thing?

Was ist das Ding da?

think · (believe) glauben, denken, (consider) meinen, finden

I think he is ready.

Ich glaube, er ist fertig.

Maddy thinks spiders are horrible. What do you think?

Maddy findet Spinnen scheußlich. Was meinst du?

(to be) thirsty · Durst haben

Polly is very thirsty.

Polly hat großen Durst.

a b c d e f g h i j k l m n o p q r s t u v w x y z

through *to* toe

through   **durch**

Mr. Bun is going out through the front door.
Herr Bun geht durch die Haustür hinaus.

throw   **werfen,**
(to someone) zu/werfen*

Anna is throwing the ball to Jack.
Anna wirft Jack den Ball zu.

Don't throw stones!
Wirf keine Steine!

thumb   **der Daumen**

This is Polly's thumb.
Das hier ist Pollys Daumen.

ticket   **die Karte,**
(train, bus) die Fahrkarte

I've bought my ticket.
Ich habe meine Fahrkarte gekauft.

tie   **binden**

Someone has tied the ribbons.
Jemand hat die Bänder gebunden.

tiger   **der Tiger**

Tigers live in Asia.
Tiger leben in Asien.

time   **(on a clock) Uhr,**
(time taken) die Zeit

What time is it?
Wie viel Uhr ist es?

I don't have much time.
Ich habe nicht viel Zeit.

tiny   **winzig**

a small cat and a tiny cat
eine kleine Katze und eine winzige Katze

tip   **die Spitze,**
das Ende

The tip of this fox's tail is white.
Dieser Fuchsschwanz hat ein weißes Ende.

the tip of the pencil
die Bleistiftspitze

toast   **der Toast**

The toast is ready.
Der Toast ist fertig.

toddler   **das Kleinkind**

Joshua is still a toddler.
Joshua ist noch ein Kleinkind.

toe   **die Zehe**

Your toes are at the end of your feet.
Die Zehen sind am Ende der Füße.

a b c d e f g h i j k l m n o p q r s **t** u v w x y z
* This is a separable verb (see page 99). 81

together   **zusammen**

Jenny and Ethan are playing together.

Jenny und Ethan spielen zusammen.

---

tonight   **heute Abend,**
(in the night) **heute Nacht**

Ich gehe heute Abend ins Theater.

She's going to the theatre tonight.

(on) top   **oben**

The kitten is on top of the desk.

Das Kätzchen sitzt oben auf dem Schreibtisch.

---

toilet   **die Toilette**

a blue toilet
eine blaue Toilette

---

tooth   **der Zahn**

Zach is showing his teeth.
Zach zeigt seine Zähne.

---

touch   **berühren**

The label says "Do not touch."

I can touch my toes.
Ich kann meine Zehen berühren.

Nicht berühren

---

tomato   **die Tomate**

a nice, ripe tomato
eine schöne, reife Tomate

---

toothbrush   **die Zahnbürste**

This is Zach's toothbrush.

Das hier ist Zachs Zahnbürste.

---

towel   **das Handtuch,**
(bath, beach) **das Badetuch**

Anna has a big, blue towel.
Anna hat ein großes, blaues Badetuch.

---

tongue   **die Zunge**

Luke is sticking his tongue out.
Luke streckt die Zunge heraus.

---

toothpaste   **die Zahnpasta**

mint flavor toothpaste

Zahnpasta mit Pfefferminzgeschmack

---

town   **die Stadt**

This is the town center.
Das ist die Stadtmitte.

a b c d e f g h i j k l m n o p q r s t u v w x y z

toy das Spielzeug, (toys) die Spielsachen

Joshua has lots of toys.

Joshua hat viele Spielsachen.

tractor der Traktor

The farmer has a red tractor.
Der Bauer hat einen roten Traktor.

train der Zug

an express train
ein Schnellzug

tree der Baum

There are lots of trees in the park.

Im Park sind viele Bäume.

truck der Lastwagen

a big, green truck
ein großer, grüner Lastwagen

Lehmanns Lastwagen

true wahr, richtig

RICHTIG ODER FALSCH?
A. Ein Ozelot ist eine Pflanzenart.
B. Pinguine können nicht fliegen.

True or false?

It's a true story.
Es ist eine wahre Geschichte.

try versuchen, (take a little) probieren

They are trying to move the package.
Sie versuchen, das Paket umzustellen.

Can I try your ice cream?
Kann ich dein Eis probieren?

T-shirt das T-Shirt

Ash is wearing a red and yellow T-shirt.
Ash trägt ein rotgelbes T-Shirt.

turkey der Truthahn

A turkey is an American bird.

Der Truthahn ist ein amerikanischer Vogel.

turn ab/biegen*, sich drehen

Jan's turning left.
Jan biegt links ab.

The wheels are turning.
Die Räder drehen sich.

TV das Fernsehen, (TV set) der Fernseher

What's on TV this evening?
Was kommt heute Abend im Fernsehen?

a new TV
ein neuer Fernseher

twin der Zwilling

Bill and Ben are twins.
Bill und Ben sind Zwillinge.

a b c d e f g h i j k l m n o p q r s t u v w x y z

* This is a separable verb (see page 99).   83

ugly — **hässlich**

This fish is ugly.
Dieser Fisch ist hässlich.

umbrella — **der Regenschirm**

Robert has a big umbrella.

Robert hat einen großen Regenschirm.

under — **unter**

The kitten is hiding under the boards.

Das Kätzchen hält sich unter den Brettern versteckt.

understand — **verstehen**

I don't understand what Ben is saying.
Ich verstehe nicht, was Ben sagt.

Bäh bäh öh!

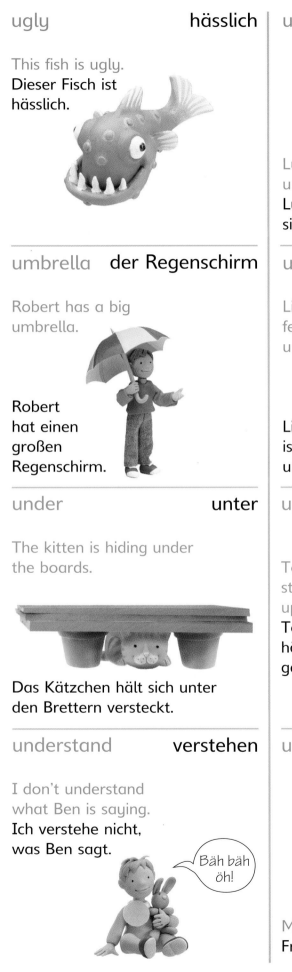

undress — **aus/ziehen*,**
(yourself) sich aus/ziehen*

Luke is undressing.
Luke zieht sich aus.

unhappy — **unglücklich**

Liddy feels very unhappy.

Liddy ist sehr unglücklich.

upright — **(person) gerade,**
(wall, pillar) senkrecht

Tony is standing upright.
Tony hält sich gerade.

The goalposts aren't upright.
Die Torpfosten sind nicht senkrecht.

upset — **(worried) aufgeregt,**
(sad) betrübt, bestürzt

Mrs. Beef is upset.
Frau Beef ist aufgeregt.

upside down — **verkehrt herum**

The picture is upside down.

Das Bild hängt verkehrt herum.

use — **benutzen**

Mr. Clack is using a saw.
Herr Clack benutzt eine Säge.

useful — **nützlich**

A wheelbarrow is very useful in the garden.
Eine Schubkarre ist im Garten sehr nützlich.

usually — **gewöhnlich,**
normalerweise

Sara usually cycles to school.
Sara fährt gewöhnlich mit dem Rad zur Schule.

Vv
vacuum cleaner *to* voice

Ww
wait *to* wake

vacuum cleaner — **der Staubsauger**

Where's the vacuum cleaner?

Wo ist der Staubsauger?

vase — **die Vase**

a vase with purple flowers in it

eine Vase mit violetten Blumen darin

vegetable — **das Gemüse**

different vegetables

verschiedene Gemüsesorten

very — **sehr**

Flora is dirty and Sally is very dirty.

Flora ist schmutzig und Sally ist sehr schmutzig.

view — **die Aussicht, der Blick**

a nice view of the country

ein schöner Blick auf die Landschaft

visit — **(person) besuchen, (place) besichtigen**

The children are visiting the museum.

Die Kinder besichtigen das Museum.

visitor — **der Gast**

The visitors are arriving.

Die Gäste kommen an.

voice — **die Stimme**

Molly has a lovely voice.

Laaaaaa!

Molly hat eine schöne Stimme.

wait — **warten**

They are waiting for the bus.

Sie warten auf den Bus.

waiter — **der Kellner**

The waiter is bringing a cup of tea.

Der Kellner bringt eine Tasse Tee.

waitress — **die Kellnerin**

The waitress is bringing two cups of coffee.

Die Kellnerin bringt zwei Tassen Kaffee.

wake — **(someone) wecken, (wake up) auf/wachen***

Sam is waking up.

Sam wacht auf.

a b c d e f g h i j k l m n o p q r s t u v w x y z

walk laufen, (go on foot) zu Fuß gehen

Danny is walking fast.
Danny läuft schnell.

He walks to school.
Er geht zu Fuß zur Schule.

wall (outside) die Mauer, (inside) die Wand

The hens are sitting on a stone wall.
Die Hühner sitzen auf einer Steinmauer.

want wollen

Jenny wants some more wagons.

Jenny will noch ein paar Waggons.

warm warm

Renata is wearing a nice, warm coat.
Renata hat einen schönen, warmen Mantel an.

wash waschen, (yourself) sich waschen

Jack is washing.
Jack wäscht sich.

washing machine die Waschmaschine

a new washing machine
eine neue Waschmaschine

watch¹ die Uhr, die Armbanduhr

Polly got a new watch for her birthday.
Polly hat zum Geburtstag eine neue Uhr bekommen.

watch² an/schauen*, an/sehen*

They are all watching the clown.

Sie schauen alle den Clown an
or **Sie sehen alle den Clown an.**

water das Wasser

Becky is playing in the water.
Becky spielt im Wasser.

wave¹ die Welle

a big wave **eine große Welle**

wave² winken, (to someone) zu/winken*

Polly is waving to her friends.
Polly winkt ihren Freunden zu.

way (route) der Weg, (method) die Art

a good way to cook eggs
eine gute Art, Eier zu kochen

the way to the village
der Weg zum Dorf

a b c d e f g h i j k l m n o p q r s t u v w x y z

wear — tragen, an/haben*

Miriam is wearing a red suit.
Miriam trägt ein rotes Kostüm *or* Miriam hat ein rotes Kostüm an.

weather — das Wetter

What's the weather like today?
Wie ist das Wetter heute?

web — (spider's) das Netz, World Wide Web das Internet

a spider's web
ein Spinnennetz

I'm searching the Web.
Ich suche im Internet.

a website
eine Internetseite *or* eine Website

week — die Woche

There are seven days in a week.
Die Woche hat sieben Tage.

Montag
Dienstag
Mittwoch
Donnerstag
Freitag
Samstag
Sonntag

well — gut

How are you?
Very well, thank you.
Wie geht's?
Danke, sehr gut.

Sara reads very well.
Sara liest sehr gut.

wet — nass

Jem the plumber is all wet.
Klempner Jem ist ganz nass.

whale — der Wal

This whale can swim very fast.
Dieser Wal kann sehr schnell schwimmen.

wheel — das Rad

a big truck wheel
ein großes Lastwagenrad

while — während

Jack is eating cake while his parents are talking.
Jack isst Kuchen, während seine Eltern sich unterhalten.

wide — breit, weit

The sofa is quite wide.
Das Sofa ist ziemlich breit.

a wide skirt
ein weiter Rock

wild — wild

These are all wild animals.
Dies sind alle wilde Tiere.

win — gewinnen

The pink cake has won first prize.
Der rosa Kuchen hat den ersten Preis gewonnen.

a b c d e f g h i j k l m n o p q r s t u v w x y z

* This is a separable verb (see page 99).

wind   der Wind

The wind is blowing.
Der Wind weht.

window   das Fenster

Look out of the window.
Schau zum Fenster hinaus!

wish   der Wunsch, (make a wish) sich etwas wünschen

The fairy can grant three wishes.
Die Fee kann drei Wünsche erfüllen.

Did you make a wish?
Hast du dir etwas gewünscht?

witch   die Hexe

There are often witches in fairy tales.
In Märchen kommen oft Hexen vor.

with   mit

Ben sleeps with his teddy bear.
Ben schläft mit seinem Teddy.

a bird with blue feet
ein Vogel mit blauen Füßen

woman   die Frau

This woman is a gardener.
Diese Frau ist Gärtnerin.

wood   das Holz, (trees) der Wald

This table is made of wood.
Dieser Tisch ist aus Holz.

There are woods beside the lake.
Neben dem See liegt ein Wald.

word   das Wort

a list of words
eine Liste mit Wörtern

Adresse
brennen
Drache
leer

work   (do a job) arbeiten, (function) funktionieren

Mick works all day.
Mick arbeitet den ganzen Tag.

This computer doesn't work.
Dieser Computer funktioniert nicht.

world   die Welt

Mr. Brand is traveling around the world.

Herr Brand macht eine Weltreise.

write   schreiben

Oliver is writing his name.
Oliver schreibt seinen Namen.

OLIVER

wrong   (incorrect) falsch, (bad) unrecht

the wrong answers
die falschen Antworten

$2 + 3 = 7$ X
$4 + 6 = 9$ X
$5 - 3 = 4$ X

It's wrong to steal.
Es ist unrecht zu stehlen.

a b c d e f g h i j k l m n o p q r s t u v w x y z

x   das Kreuz, (in math) x

Put an "x" in the box.
Mach ein Kreuz in das Kästchen.

$$2 \times 2 = 4$$

(two times two equals four)
(zwei mal zwei ist vier)

Xmas   Weihnachten

Merry Xmas!

Frohe Weihnachten!

x-ray   das Röntgenbild, (have an x-ray) geröntgt werden

The x-ray shows Robert's skeleton.
Das Röntgenbild zeigt Roberts Skelett.

Robert is having an x-ray.
Robert wird geröntgt.

xylophone   das Xylophon

This xylophone has six notes.
Dieses Xylophon hat sechs Töne.

yawn   gähnen

Sam's yawning.
Sam gähnt.

year   das Jahr

Flora is five years old. Annie is a year older.
Flora ist fünf Jahre alt. Annie ist ein Jahr älter.

yet   noch

Ben can't walk yet.
Ben kann noch nicht laufen.

young   jung, (children) klein

young people
junge Leute

young children
kleine Kinder

zebra   das Zebra

Zebras live in Africa.
Zebras leben in Afrika.

zero   null

Five take away five equals zero.
Fünf weniger fünf ist null.

$$5 - 5 = 0$$

zipper   der Reißverschluss

The zipper is half open.
Der Reißverschluss ist halb offen.

zoo   der Zoo, der Tiergarten

There's a panda at the zoo.
Im Zoo ist ein Panda.

a b c d e f g h i j k l m n o p q r s t u v w x y z

Colors

Farben

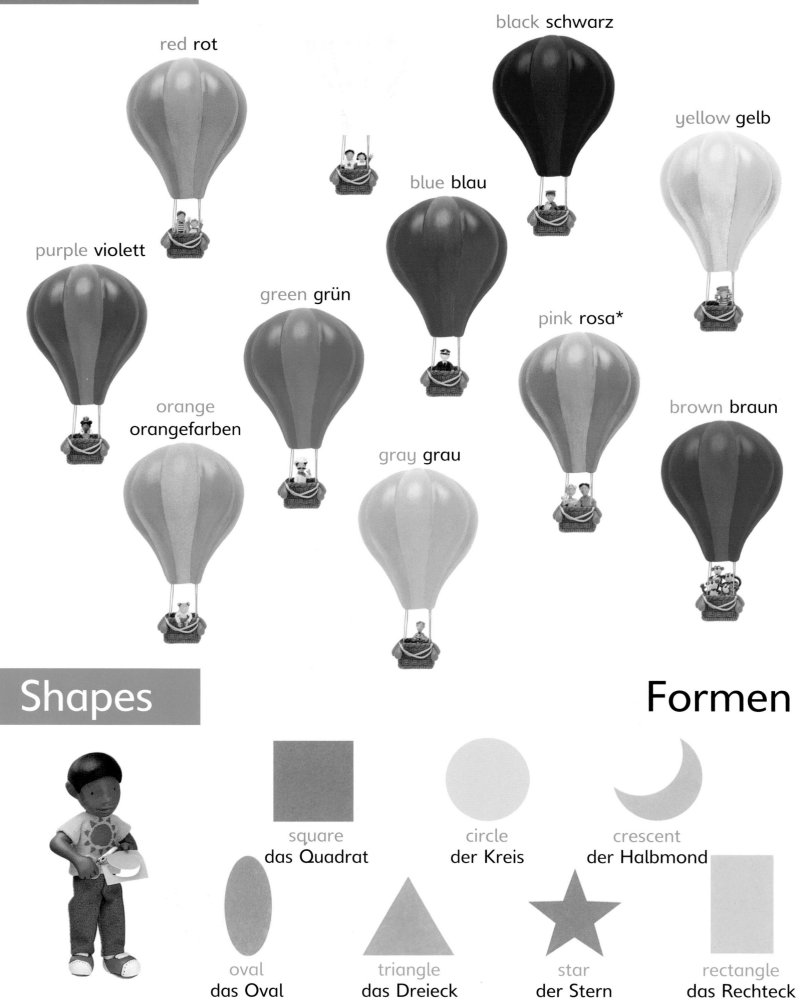

white **weiß**

black **schwarz**

red **rot**

yellow **gelb**

blue **blau**

purple **violett**

green **grün**

pink **rosa***

orange
orangefarben

gray **grau**

brown **braun**

Shapes

Formen

square
das Quadrat

circle
der Kreis

crescent
der Halbmond

oval
das Oval

triangle
das Dreieck

star
der Stern

rectangle
das Rechteck

* This word is always spelled the same. You don't need to add on any adjective endings.

Numbers

Zahlen

1st 1.	2nd 2.	3rd 3.	4th 4.	5th 5.	6th 6.	7th 7.	8th 8.	9th 9.	10th 10.
erst-*		dritt-*		fünft-*		siebt-*		neunt-*	
	zweit-*		viert-*		sechst-*		acht-*		zehnt-*

1	eins	
2	zwei	
3	drei	
4	vier	
5	fünf	
6	sechs	
7	sieben	
8	acht	
9	neun	
10	zehn	
11	elf	
12	zwölf	
13	dreizehn	
14	vierzehn	
15	fünfzehn	
16	sechzehn	
17	siebzehn	
18	achtzehn	
19	neunzehn	
20	zwanzig	

30	40	50	60	70	80	90	100	1000
dreißig	vierzig	fünfzig	sechzig	siebzig	achtzig	neunzig	hundert	tausend

* You need to add an adjective ending to these words (see page 4): my first day at school – mein erster Schultag.

Days and months   Die Tage und Monate

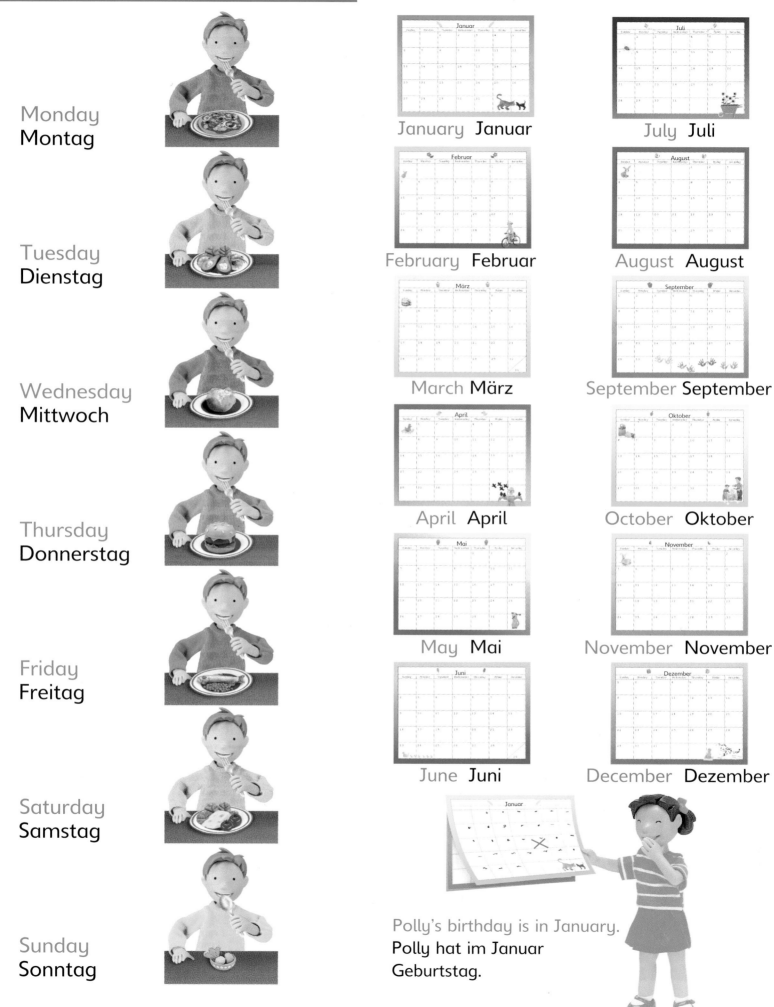

Monday
Montag

Tuesday
Dienstag

Wednesday
Mittwoch

Thursday
Donnerstag

Friday
Freitag

Saturday
Samstag

Sunday
Sonntag

January **Januar**

February **Februar**

March **März**

April **April**

May **Mai**

June **Juni**

July **Juli**

August **August**

September **September**

October **Oktober**

November **November**

December **Dezember**

Polly's birthday is in January.
**Polly hat im Januar
Geburtstag.**

Die Jahreszeiten

Spring der Frühling

Summer der Sommer

Fall der Herbst

Winter der Winter

Family

Die Familie

Polly's photo album
Pollys Fotoalbum

sister, brother
**die Schwester,
der Bruder**

father
der Vater

mother
die Mutter

Dad
Vati

Mom
Mutti

son
der Sohn

daughter
die Tochter

grandmother
die Großmutter

grandfather
der Großvater

Granny
Oma

grandchildren
die Enkelkinder

Grandpa
Opa

Dad and his brother
Vati und sein Bruder

baby
das Baby

aunt
die Tante

(girl) cousin
die Cousine*

uncle
der Onkel

grandparents
die Großeltern

children
die Kinder

parents
die Eltern

* boy cousin would be *der Cousin*.

94

Words we use a lot

On these pages you'll find some words that are useful for making sentences. Remember that in German some words can change their spelling, depending on whether the word that follows is masculine, feminine, neuter or plural, and on what part the word plays in a sentence (see page 4).

about	(story) über, (roughly) ungefähr
across	über
again	wieder or noch einmal
almost	fast
also	auch
always	immer
and	und
another	noch ein (eine, ein)
at	(a place) an or bei (a time) um
because	weil
but	aber
by	(beside) neben, (done by) von, (by car, bus) mit
each or every	jeder (jede, jedes)
everybody or everyone	alle or jeder
everything	alles
everywhere	überall
for	für
from	von
he	er
her	sie, (to or for her) ihr, (belonging to her) ihr (ihre, ihr, ihre)
here	hier, (to here) hierher
him	ihn, (to or for him) ihm
I	ich
if	wenn

in, into	in
it	er (sie, es)
maybe	vielleicht
me	mich, (to or for me) mir
never	nie
no	(not yes) nein, (not one) kein (keine, kein, keine)
no one	niemand
nothing	nichts
nowhere	nirgends
often	oft
on	(something flat) auf, (something vertical) an
or	oder
she	sie
since	(time) seit, (because) da
so	(so big) so, (because of this) also
some	(of one thing) etwas, (several things) ein paar or einige
somebody or someone	jemand
something	etwas
sometimes	manchmal
somewhere	irgendwo
them	sie, (to or for them) ihnen
then	(next) dann, (at that time) damals
there	da or dort, (to there) dahin or dorthin

they	sie
through	durch
to	zu, (a town or country) nach, (in order to) um . . . zu
today	heute
tomorrow	morgen
too	(also) auch, (too much, too hot) zu
under	unter
until	bis
us	uns
we	wir
what	was
where	wo
with	mit
without	ohne
yes	ja
yesterday	gestern
you	du, ihr or Sie*, (to or for you) dir, euch or Ihnen

* For the difference between *du*, *ihr* and *Sie*, see page 4.

95

This, that

On page 3, you can see how the word for "the" changes, depending on whether a noun is masculine, feminine or neuter. The word for "this" is *dieser* and it changes in a similar way:

the boy	der Junge
this boy	dieser Junge
the woman	die Frau
this woman	diese Frau
the house	das Haus
this house	dieses Haus

When you are talking about more than one of something (plurals), the word for "these" is *diese* for masculine, feminine and neuter nouns:

these boys	diese Jungen
these women	diese Frauen
these houses	diese Häuser

Sometimes you will see different endings. This is because the endings change depending on what part "this thing" or "these things" are playing in a sentence:

This apple tastes good.
Dieser Apfel schmeckt gut.

Do you want this apple?
Willst du diesen Apfel?

The German word for "that" is *jener*. It changes in a similar way to *dieser*.

that boy	jener Junge
that woman	jene Frau
that house	jenes Haus

The word for "those" is *jene*:

those boys	jene Jungen
those women	jene Frauen
those houses	jene Häuser

My, your, his, her

In German, the words for "my," "your," "his," "her," "our" and "their" change slightly, depending on whether the noun that follows is masculine, feminine, neuter or plural. The word for "my" is *mein*. Here's how it changes:

my brother	mein Bruder
my mother	meine Mutter
my house	mein Haus
my parents	meine Eltern

If you're talking to a younger person or someone you know very well, the word for "your" is *dein*. If you're talking to two or more people you know very well, it's *euer*. And if you're talking to one or more people you don't know so well, it's *Ihr*.

your brother
dein Bruder, euer Bruder *or* Ihr Bruder
your mother
deine Mutter, eure Mutter *or* Ihre Mutter
your house
dein Haus, euer Haus *or* Ihr Haus
your parents
deine Eltern, eure Eltern *or* Ihre Eltern

The word for "his" is *sein*:

his brother	sein Bruder
his mother	seine Mutter
his house	sein Haus
his parents	seine Eltern

The word for "her" and "their" is *ihr*. And the word for "our" is *unser*:

her brother *or* their brother	ihr Bruder
her mother *or* their mother	ihre Mutter
our house	unser Haus
our parents	unsere Eltern

Making sentences

To make sentences in German, you often put the words in the same order as in an English sentence:

The baker sells fresh bread.
Der Bäcker verkauft frisches Brot.

The bus is going into town.
Der Bus fährt in die Stadt.

But German word order is sometimes very different from English. In German, the verb (or "doing" word) is usually the second idea in the sentence. So, if you start a sentence with a word or phrase such as "today" or "in the summer," the verb must come next:

Today we're going to the park.
Heute gehen wir in den Park.

In the summer I play tennis.
Im Sommer spiele ich Tennis.

Sometimes, you have to put the verb at the end of a sentence, for example, after the words *wenn* ("if" or "when"), *weil* ("because"), *während* ("while"), *bis* ("until") and *da* ("since"):

I wear gloves when it's cold.
Ich trage Handschuhe, wenn es kalt ist.

Liddy is sad because she misses her mom.
Liddy ist traurig, weil sie ihre Mutti vermisst.

Often, a sentence has two verbs, with the second one in the infinitive (the "to" form): "I want to go home." In German, the second verb goes to the end of the sentence:

I want to play soccer.
Ich will Fußball spielen.

I have to do my homework.
Ich muss meine Hausaufgaben machen.

Can I have some more strawberries?
Kann ich noch Erdbeeren haben?

More and most

In English, when you compare things, you often add "er" to an adjective: "A mouse is smaller than a rabbit." Other times, you use "more": "My puzzle is more difficult than yours." In German, you always add *-er* to the adjective:

Cars are faster than bicycles.
Autos sind schneller als Fahrräder.

With some short adjectives, you need to add an umlaut (¨) as well:

Olivia is taller than Joshua.
Olivia ist größer als Joshua.

Joshua is older than Ben.
Joshua ist älter als Ben.

When you compare several things, in English you usually add "est" to the adjective or use "most": "the tallest tree" or "the most delicious cake." In German, you add *-ste* to the adjective:

the fastest car
das schnellste Auto

Again, with some short adjectives, you need to add an umlaut (¨):

the longest river
der längste Fluss

the youngest baby
das jüngste Baby

As in English, there are special words for:

better   besser
the best   der, die *or* das beste

My plane is better than your car.
Mein Flugzeug ist besser als dein Auto.

the best pupil
der beste Schüler *or* die beste Schülerin

Making questions

To make a question in German, you put the verb before the subject of the sentence and add a question mark:

Is the bus going into town?
Fährt der Bus in die Stadt?

Is the kitten behind the flowerpot?
Ist das Kätzchen hinter dem Blumentopf?

You can also make questions beginning with question words, such as:

Who..?	Wer..?
Which..?	Welcher..?, Welche..?, Welches..? or Welche..?
What..?	Was..?
Where..?	Wo..?
When..?	Wann..?
Why..?	Warum..?
How..? or What...like?	Wie..?
How much..?	Wie viel..?
How many..?	Wie viele..?

For example:

How many CDs do you have?
Wie viele CDs hast du?

What's the weather like today?
Wie ist das Wetter heute?

And there are some other useful words for questions, which begin with "any–" in English:

anybody or anyone	jemand
anything	etwas
anywhere	irgendwo

For example:

Is anybody in the classroom?
Ist jemand im Klassenzimmer?

Do you need anything?
Brauchst du etwas?

Have you seen my glasses anywhere?
Hast du irgendwo meine Brille gesehen?

Negative sentences

A negative sentence is a "not" sentence, such as "I'm not tired." To make a sentence negative in German, you add the word *nicht*:

I'm not tired.
Ich bin nicht müde.

This bus isn't going into town.
Dieser Bus fährt nicht in die Stadt.

The kitten isn't under the table.
Das Kätzchen ist nicht unter dem Tisch.

To say "no . . .", "not a . . ." or "not any . . .", you use *kein* with masculine nouns, *keine* with feminine nouns, *kein* with neuter nouns and *keine* with plural nouns. For example:

That's not a dog.
Das ist kein Hund.

She's not wearing a cap.
Sie trägt keine Mütze.

We don't eat meat *or* We eat no meat.
Wir essen kein Fleisch.

I have no pets *or* I don't have any pets.
Ich habe keine Haustiere.

Here are some more useful words for negative sentences:

nobody *or* no one	niemand
nothing	nichts
never	nie

This is how they're used:

There is nobody at home
  or There isn't anybody at home.
Niemand ist zu Hause.

I have nothing to eat
  or I don't have anything to eat.
Ich habe nichts zu essen.

The train is never late
  or The train isn't ever late.
Der Zug kommt nie zu spät.

Verbs

The next few pages list the verbs (or "doing" words) that appear in the main part of the dictionary. Page 4 explains a little about verbs in German, and how the endings change for "I," "you," "he," "she," and so on.

To use a verb in the present (the form you use to talk about things that are happening now), you start with the infinitive (the "to" form) and take off the -en. Then you add these endings:

ich - I	-e
du - you (singular)	-st
er, sie, es - he, she, it	-t
wir - we	-en
ihr - you (plural)	-t
sie - they	-en
Sie - you (polite)	-en

For example, the verb "to do" is *machen*. To say "I do," you take off the -en and add -e (*ich mache*). To say "he does," you add -t (*er macht*), and so on. On the following pages, you'll find the infinitive (the "to" form) and the "he, she *or* it" form of each verb.

Some verbs change their spelling slightly in the "you" (*du*) form and in the "he, she *or* it" form. These verbs are listed with the "I" form as well, so you can see how the spelling changes:

to speak	sprechen
I speak	ich spreche
he speaks	er spricht

A few verbs, such as the verbs *sein* ("to be") and *haben* ("to have"), don't follow the normal pattern. These verbs are listed in full.

Reflexive verbs

Reflexive verbs are a special kind of verb. They are often used where in English you would use ". . . myself," ". . . yourself," and so on. The main part of the verb works just like other verbs, but you need to add an extra word depending on who is doing the action. For example, *sich waschen* ("to wash yourself") is formed like this:

I wash myself	ich wasche mich
you wash yourself	du wäschst dich
he washes himself, she washes herself *or* it washes itself	er, sie *or* es wäscht sich
we wash ourselves	wir waschen uns
you wash yourselves	ihr wascht euch
they wash themselves	sie waschen sich
you wash yourself *or* you wash yourselves	Sie waschen sich

Separable verbs

Some German verbs, called separable verbs, split up when you use them in a sentence. For example, the verb "to open" is *aufmachen*, but when you use it in a sentence it looks like this:

She opens the door.
Sie macht die Tür auf.

Please open the window!
Mach bitte das Fenster auf!

In the main part of the dictionary and in the verb list on the following pages, separable verbs are shown like this: *auf/machen*. The slash shows you where the verb splits.

Verbs

ab/biegen — to turn
er biegt ab (left, right)

ab/lecken — to lick (of
er leckt ab animals)

ab/schreiben — to copy
er schreibt ab (writing)

sich ab/trocknen — to
er trocknet dry
  sich ab yourself

sich amüsieren — to
er amüsiert enjoy
  sich yourself

an/fangen — to start
ich fange an
er fängt an

angeln — to fish
ich angle
er angelt

an/haben* — to wear
ich habe an
er hat an

an/halten — to stop
ich halte an
er hält an

an/kommen — to arrive
er kommt an

an/schauen — to look (at),
er schaut an to watch

an/sehen — to look (at),
ich sehe an to watch
er sieht an

antworten — to answer,
er antwortet to reply

an/ziehen — to dress
er zieht an (someone)

sich an/ziehen — to dress
er zieht (yourself)
  sich an

arbeiten — to work
er arbeitet

atmen — to breathe
er atmet

auf/bewahren — to keep
er bewahrt auf (store)

auf/hören — to stop
er hört auf

auf/machen — to open
er macht auf

auf/stehen — to stand up
er steht auf

auf/wachen — to wake up
er wacht auf

auf/wärmen — to heat
er wärmt auf (food)

aus/geben — to spend
ich gebe aus (money)
er gibt aus

aus/rutschen — to slip
er rutscht aus

aus/schneiden — to cut
er schneidet aus out

aus/schütten — to spill
er schüttet aus

aus/suchen — to choose,
er sucht aus to pick

aus/ziehen — to
er zieht aus undress
(someone)

sich aus/ziehen — to
er zieht undress
  sich aus (yourself)

backen — to bake
ich backe
er backt or er bäckt

balancieren — to balance
er balanciert

bauen — to build
er baut

sich bedanken — to thank
er bedankt sich

bedeuten — to mean
er bedeutet

sich beeilen — to hurry,
er beeilt sich to rush

sich befassen mit — to
er befasst study
  sich mit (a topic)

befühlen — to feel
er befühlt (touch)

begegnen — to meet
er begegnet (by chance)

beginnen — to begin
er beginnt

behalten — to keep
ich behalte
er behält

beißen — to bite
er beißt

bellen — to bark
er bellt

bemerken — to notice
er bemerkt

benutzen — to use
er benutzt

berühren — to touch
er berührt

besichtigen — to visit
er besichtigt (a place)

besuchen — to visit
er besucht (a person)

sich bewegen — to move
er bewegt (yourself)
  sich

bezahlen — to pay for
er bezahlt

binden — to tie
er bindet

blasen — to blow
ich blase
er bläst

bleiben — to stay
er bleibt (remain)

braten — to fry
ich brate
er brät

brauchen — to need
er braucht

brechen — to break
ich breche
er bricht

brennen — to burn
er brennt

bringen — to bring
er bringt

buchstabieren — to spell
er buchstabiert

bügeln — to iron
er bügelt

danken — to thank
er dankt

denken — to think
er denkt

deuten — to point
er deutet

sich drehen — to turn
er dreht sich (around)

drücken — to press
er drückt

eilen — to rush
er eilt

ein/frieren — to freeze
er friert ein (food)

ein/laden — to invite
ich lade ein
er lädt ein

ein/laufen — to shrink
er läuft ein (clothes)
sie laufen ein

entdecken — to spot
er entdeckt

entkommen — to escape
er entkommt

sich erinnern an — to remember
er erinnert
  sich an

erklären — to explain
er erklärt

erzählen — to tell
er erzählt (a story)

essen — to eat
ich esse
er isst

* See *haben* for the other parts of this verb. 100

fahren — to go (by car, boat, train),
ich fahre
er fährt — to drive

fallen — to fall
ich falle
er fällt

fallen lassen — to drop
ich lasse fallen
er lässt fallen

fangen — to catch
ich fange
er fängt

fegen — to sweep
er fegt

fertig machen — to finish
er macht fertig

fest/machen — to fix
er macht fest (attach)

finden — to find, to think
er findet (consider)

flicken — to mend,
er flickt — to repair

fliegen — to fly
er fliegt

fragen — to ask
er fragt

fressen — to eat
ich fresse (of animals)
er frisst

sich freuen — to be glad
er freut sich

frieren — to freeze
er friert

fühlen — to feel
er fühlt (touch)

sich fühlen — to feel
er fühlt sich (happy, sad)

führen — to lead
er führt

füllen — to fill
er füllt

funktionieren — to work
er funktioniert (function)

füttern — to feed
er füttert

gähnen — to yawn
er gähnt

geben — to give
ich gebe
er gibt

gefrieren — to freeze
er gefriert

gegenüber/stehen — to face
er steht gegenüber

gehen — to go
er geht (on foot)

gehören — to belong
er gehört

gewinnen — to win
er gewinnt

glauben — to think
er glaubt

graben — to dig
ich grabe
er gräbt

haben — to have
ich habe
du hast
er, sie, es hat
wir haben
ihr habt
sie haben
Sie haben

halten — to hold
ich halte
er hält

hängen — to hang
er hängt

hassen — to hate
er hasst

heizen — to heat
er heizt (a room)

helfen — to help
ich helfe
er hilft

heran/reichen — to reach
er reicht heran

hinauf/steigen — to climb
er steigt hinauf

hin/fallen — to fall
ich falle hin — down
er fällt hin

sich hin/knien — to kneel
er kniet sich hin (down)

sich hin/legen — to lie
er legt sich hin — down

sich hin/setzen — to sit
er setzt sich hin — down

hinzu/fügen — to add
er fügt hinzu (things)

hoch/heben — to lift
er hebt hoch

hören — to hear
er hört

hüpfen — to hop
er hüpft

jagen — to chase,
er jagt — to hunt

jonglieren — to juggle
er jongliert

jucken — to itch
er juckt

kämpfen — to fight
er kämpft

kaputt/machen — to
er macht — break
kaputt (a machine)

kaufen — to buy
er kauft

kehren — to sweep
er kehrt

kennen — to know
er kennt (people)

kicken — to kick
er kickt

kleben — to stick
er klebt

klingeln — to ring
er klingelt

klopfen — to knock
er klopft (on door)

knien — to kneel
er kniet (be kneeling)

kochen — to cook
er kocht

kommen — to come
er kommt

können — to be able
ich kann (I can, etc.)
du kannst
er, sie, es kann
wir können
ihr könnt
sie können
Sie können

krabbeln — to crawl
er krabbelt (baby)

kriechen — to crawl
er kriecht

küssen — to kiss
er küsst

lächeln — to smile
er lächelt

lachen — to laugh
er lacht

lassen — to let
ich lasse
er lässt

laufen — to walk,
ich laufe — to run,
er läuft — to go on foot

läuten — to ring
er läutet

leben — to live
er lebt (be alive)

lecken — to lick
er leckt

legen — to put
er legt

lernen — to learn,
er lernt — to study

lesen — to read
ich lese
er liest

101

Verbs

lieben er liebt	to love	sich neigen er neigt sich	to lean (to one side)	rufen er ruft	to call, to shout	sehen ich sehe er sieht	to see
liegen er liegt	to lie (be lying)	nennen er nennt	to call (name)	rutschen er rutscht	to slide	sein ich bin du bist	to be
liegen lassen ich lasse liegen er lässt liegen	to leave (some- thing)	nicken er nickt	to nod	sagen er sagt	to say, to tell	er, sie, es ist wir sind ihr seid	
lügen er lügt	to lie (tell a lie)	öffnen er öffnet	to open	schaukeln er schaukelt	to swing	sie sind Sie sind	
machen er macht	to make, to do	parken er parkt	to park	schenken er schenkt	to give (as a gift)	setzen er setzt	to put
malen er malt	to paint (a picture)	passen er passt	to fit	schicken er schickt	to send	singen er singt	to sing
meinen er meint	to think (consider)	passieren es passiert	to happen	schieben er schiebt	to push	sinken er sinkt	to sink
messen ich messe er misst	to measure	pflücken er pflückt	to pick (fruit or flowers)	schlafen ich schlafe er schläft	to sleep, to be asleep	sitzen er sitzt	to sit
mischen er mischt	to mix	planen er plant	to plan	schlagen ich schlage er schlägt	to hit	sparen er spart	to save (time, money)
mit/nehmen ich nehme mit er nimmt mit	to take	probieren er probiert	to try, to taste	sich schlagen ich schlage mich er schlägt sich	to fight	spielen er spielt	to play
mögen ich mag du magst	to like	putzen er putzt	to clean	schleichen er schleicht	to creep	sprechen ich spreche er spricht	to speak, to talk
er, sie, es mag wir mögen ihr mögt sie mögen Sie mögen		quaken er quakt	to quack	schließen er schließt	to close, to shut	springen er springt	to jump, to dive
		raten ich rate er rät	to guess	schmecken er schmeckt	to taste	spritzen er spritzt	to splash
müssen ich muss du musst er, sie, es muss	to have to, to need to (I must, etc.)	regnen es regnet	to rain	schneiden er schneidet	to cut	stechen ich steche er sticht	to sting
wir müssen ihr müsst sie müssen Sie müssen		reichen er reicht	to pass (give)	schneien es schneit	to snow	stecken er steckt	to put (inside)
nach/ahmen er ahmt nach	to copy (actions)	reiten er reitet	to ride (a horse)	schreiben er schreibt	to write	stehen er steht	to stand
nähen er näht	to sew	rennen er rennt	to run	schreien er schreit	to shout	stellen er stellt	to put
		reparieren er repariert	to fix, to mend	schütteln er schüttelt	to shake	sterben ich sterbe er stirbt	to die
nehmen ich nehme er nimmt	to take	retten er rettet	to save, to rescue	schweben er schwebt	to float (in air)	stoßen ich stoße er stößt	to bump
		riechen er riecht	to smell	schwimmen er schwimmt	to swim, to float		

streichen — to paint
er streicht — (a room)

sich stützen — to lean
er stützt sich — (on)

suchen — to search
er sucht

tanzen — to dance
er tanzt

tauchen — to dive
er taucht

teilen — to share
er teilt

töten — to kill
er tötet

tragen — to carry,
ich trage — to wear
er trägt

träumen — to dream
er träumt

sich treffen — to meet
ich treffe mich
er trifft sich

trinken — to drink
er trinkt

trocknen — to dry
er trocknet

tun — to do
ich tue
du tust
er, sie, es tut
wir tun
ihr tut
sie tun
Sie tun

überqueren — to cross
er überquert

umarmen — to hug
er umarmt

um/stellen — to move
er stellt um — (an object)

um/stoßen — to knock
ich stoße um — (over)
er stößt um

unter/gehen — to sink
er geht unter

sich unterhalten — to talk
ich unterhalte
  mich
er unterhält sich

unterschreiben — to sign
er unterschreibt

sich verabschieden — to
er verabschiedet — say
  sich — goodbye

verbinden — to join
er verbindet — (attach)

verbrennen — to burn
er verbrennt

verbringen — to spend
er verbringt — (time)

vergessen — to forget
ich vergesse
er vergisst

verkaufen — to sell
er verkauft

verlassen — to leave
ich verlasse — (a place,
er verlässt — a person)

verlieren — to lose
er verliert

vermissen — to miss
er vermisst — (someone)

verpassen — to miss
er verpasst — (train, bus)

verrühren — to stir,
er verrührt — to mix

verschütten — to spill
er verschüttet

verschwinden
  — to disappear
er verschwindet

versprechen — to promise
ich verspreche
er verspricht

verspritzen — to splash
er verspritzt

verstecken — to hide
er versteckt — (things)

sich verstecken — to hide
er versteckt — (yourself)
  sich

verstehen — to understand
er versteht

versuchen — to try
er versucht

voran/gehen — to lead (go
er geht voran — ahead)

vorbei/gehen — to pass
er geht vorbei — (go past)

wachsen — to grow
ich wachse — (get bigger)
er wächst

wählen — to choose
er wählt

warten — to wait
er wartet

waschen — to wash
ich wasche
er wäscht

sich waschen — to wash
ich wasche — (yourself)
  mich
er wäscht sich

wecken — to wake
er weckt — (someone)

weg/nehmen — to take
ich nehme weg — (away)
er nimmt weg

weh/tun* — to hurt
er tut weh

weinen — to cry
er weint

werden — to become
ich werde
du wirst
er, sie, es wird
wir werden
ihr werdet
sie werden
Sie werden

werfen — to throw
ich werfe
er wirft

winken — to wave
er winkt

wissen — to know
ich weiß — (facts)
du weißt
er, sie, es, weiß
wir wissen
ihr wisst
sie wissen
Sie wissen

wohnen — to live
er wohnt

wollen — to want
ich will
du willst
er, sie, es will
wir wollen
ihr wollt
sie wollen
Sie wollen

zahlen — to pay
er zahlt

zeichnen — to draw
er zeichnet

zeigen — to show,
er zeigt — to point

zelten — to camp
er zeltet

zerbrechen — to break
ich zerbreche
er zerbricht

ziehen — to pull, to grow
er zieht — (cultivate)

zu/machen — to close,
er macht zu — to shut

zusammen/falten
  — to fold
er faltet zusammen

zusammen/passen
  — to match
es passt zusammen

zusammen/zählen
  — to add
er zählt — (numbers)
  zusammen

zu/werfen — to throw
ich werfe zu — (to
er wirft zu — someone)

zu/winken — to wave (to
er winkt zu — someone)

* See *tun* for the other parts of this verb.   103

Complete German word list

Plurals of nouns are shown in parentheses. Nouns that don't change their spelling in the plural are shown like this: der Eimer (-)

ab/biegen	to turn (left or right)
der Abend (-e)	evening
das Abendessen (-)	dinner
abends	in the evening
aber	but
ab/lecken	to lick (of animals)
ab/schreiben	to copy (writing)
sich ab/trocknen	to dry yourself
acht	eight
acht-	eighth
achtzehn	eighteen
achtzig	eighty
der Adler (-)	eagle
die Adresse (-n)	address
der Affe (-n)	ape, monkey
alle	all, everybody, everyone
allein	alone
alles	everything
das Alphabet (-e)	alphabet
als	than, when (in past)
also	so (because of this)
alt	old
die Ameise (-n)	ant
sich amüsieren	to enjoy yourself
an	at (a place), on (something vertical)
die Ananas (-se)	pineapple
anbrennen lassen	to burn (food)
ander-	other
an/fangen	to start
angeln	to fish
Angst haben	to be afraid
an/haben	to wear
an/halten	to stop
an/kommen	to arrive, to reach
an/schauen	to look (at), to watch
an/sehen	to look (at), to watch
an sich drücken	to hug (toy, animal)
die Antwort (-en)	answer
antworten	to answer, to reply
an . . . vorbei	past
die Anzahl	number (amount)
an/ziehen	to dress (someone)
sich an/ziehen	to dress (yourself)
der Apfel (Äpfel)	apple
April	April
arbeiten	to work
das Arbeitszimmer (-)	study
arm	poor
der Arm (-e)	arm
die Armbanduhr (-en)	watch
der Ärmel (-)	sleeve
die Art (-en)	kind, sort, way (method)
artig	good (well-behaved)
der Arzt (Ärzte)	doctor (man)
die Ärztin (-nen)	doctor (woman)
der Astronaut (-en)	astronaut (man)
die Astronautin (-nen)	astronaut (woman)
atmen	to breathe
auch	also, too
auf	on (something flat)
auf/bewahren	to keep (store)
auf einmal	suddenly
aufgeregt	upset (worried)
auf/hören	to stop (doing something)
auf/machen	to open
auf/stehen	to stand up
auf/wachen	to wake up
auf/wärmen	to heat (food)
auf Wiedersehen	goodbye
das Auge (-n)	eye
August	August
aus/geben	to spend (money)
aus/machen	to matter, to turn off
aus/rutschen	to slip
aus/schneiden	to cut out
aus/schütten	to spill
außen	outside (outdoors)
außerhalb	outside (something)
die Aussicht (-en)	view
aus/suchen	to choose, to pick
aus/ziehen	to undress (someone)
sich aus/ziehen	to undress (yourself)
das Auto (-s)	car
das Baby (-s)	baby
backen	to bake
der Bäcker (-)	baker (man)
die Bäckerin (-nen)	baker (woman)
der Badeanzug (Badeanzüge)	swimsuit
das Badetuch (Badetücher)	towel (bath, beach)
die Badewanne (-n)	bathtub
der Bagger (-)	digger
der Bahnhof (Bahnhöfe)	station
balancieren	to balance
bald	soon
der Ball (Bälle)	ball
die Balletttänzerin (-nen)	ballerina
der Ballon (-s)	(hot-air) balloon
die Banane (-n)	banana
das Band (Bänder)	ribbon
die Band (-s)	band (music)
die Bank (-en)	bank
der Bär (-en)	bear
der Bart (Bärte)	beard
bauen	to build
der Bauer (-n)	farmer
der Bauernhof (Bauernhöfe)	farm
der Baum (Bäume)	tree
der Baumstamm (Baumstämme)	log
sich bedanken	to thank
bedeuten	to mean
sich beeilen	to hurry, to rush
sich befassen mit	to study (a topic)
befühlen	to feel (touch)
begegnen	to meet (by chance)
beginnen	to begin
behalten	to keep
bei	at (a place)
das Bein (-e)	leg
beißen	to bite
das belegte Brot	sandwich
bellen	to bark
bemerken	to notice
benutzen	to use
bereit	ready
der Berg (-e)	mountain
berühren	to touch
beschäftigt	busy
besichtigen	to visit (a place)
besonder-	special
bestimmt	special, certain
bestürzt	upset (sad)
besuchen	to visit, to see (visit)
betrübt	upset (sad)
das Bett (-en)	bed
das Bettlaken (-)	sheet (on bed)
sich bewegen	to move (yourself)
bezahlen	to pay for
die Biene (-n)	bee
das Bild (-er)	picture
billig	cheap
binden	to tie
der Bindfaden	string
die Birne (-n)	pear
bis	until
bitte	please
blasen	to blow
blass	pale
das Blatt (Blätter)	leaf, sheet (of paper)
blau	blue
bleiben	to stay (remain)
der Bleistift (-e)	pencil
der Blick (-e)	view
die Blockflöte (-n)	recorder
bloß	only
die Blume (-n)	flower
der Blumenkohl (-e)	cauliflower
der Boden (Böden)	floor, ground
die Bohne (-n)	bean
das Boot (-e)	boat
böse	angry
braten	to fry
brauchen	to need
braun	brown
brav	good (well-behaved)
brechen	to break
breit	wide
brennen	to burn
der Brief (-e)	letter
die Briefmarke (-n)	stamp
die Brille (-n)	glasses
bringen	to bring
das Brot (-e)	bread
die Brücke (-n)	bridge

der Bruder (Brüder)	brother
das Buch (Bücher)	book
buchstabieren	to spell
das Bügeleisen (-)	iron
bügeln	to iron
die Burg (-en)	castle
die Bürste (-n)	brush
der Bus (-se)	bus
der Busch (Büsche)	bush
die Butter	butter
das Café (-s)	café
die CD (-s)	CD
der Clown (-s)	clown
der Computer (-)	computer
der Cousin (-s)	cousin (boy)
die Cousine (-n)	cousin (girl)
da	there, since (because)
das Dach (Dächer)	roof
dahin	(to) there
damals	then (at that time)
die Dame (-n)	lady
danach	next (after that)
danken	to thank
dann	then, next
das Datum (Daten)	date
der Daumen (-)	thumb
die Decke (-n)	blanket
der Deckel (-)	lid
der Delphin (-e)	dolphin
denken	to think
der-, die-, dasselbe	the same
deuten	to point
Dezember	December
dick	fat
Dienstag	Tuesday
das Ding (-e)	thing
der Dinosaurier (-)	dinosaur
Donnerstag	Thursday
dort	there
dorthin	(to) there
der Drache (-n)	dragon
der Drachen (-)	kite
draußen	outside
der Dreck	mess, dirt
sich drehen	to turn (around)
drei	three
das Dreieck (-e)	triangle
dreißig	thirty
dreizehn	thirteen
dritt-	third
drücken	to press
der Dschungel (-)	jungle
dunkel	dark
dünn	thin
durch	through
das Durcheinander	mess (untidy)
Durst haben	to be thirsty
die Dusche (-n)	shower (for washing)

echt	real (not artificial)
das Ei (-er)	egg
das Eichhörnchen (-)	squirrel
eigen	own
eilen	to rush (move quickly)
der Eimer (-)	bucket
ein/frieren	to freeze (food)
einige	some
ein/laden	to invite
die Einladung (-en)	invitation
ein/laufen	to shrink (clothes)
einmal	once
eins	one
das Eis	ice, ice cream
der Elefant (-en)	elephant
elf	eleven
der Ellbogen (-)	elbow
die Eltern	parents
die E-Mail	email
das Ende (-n)	end, tip (of tail)
eng	narrow
der Engel (-)	angel
das Enkelkind (-er)	grandchild
entdecken	to spot
die Ente (-n)	duck
das Entenküken (-)	duckling
entkommen	to escape
die Erbse (-n)	pea
die Erdbeere (-n)	strawberry
die Erde	earth, soil
die Erdnuss (Erdnüsse)	peanut
sich erinnern an	to remember
die Erkältung (-en)	cold
erklären	to explain
erst-	first
der Erwachsene	adult, grown-up
erzählen	to tell (a story)
der Esel (-)	donkey
essen	to eat
das Essen (-)	food, meal
etwas	something, some, anything
etwas gegen . . . haben	to mind
die Eule (-n)	owl
die Fahne (-n)	flag
fahren	to go, to drive, to ride (a bicycle)
die Fahrkarte (-n)	ticket (train, bus)
das Fahrrad (Fahrräder)	bicycle
die Fahrt (-en)	journey
fallen	to fall
fallen lassen	to drop
der Fallschirm (-e)	parachute
falsch	wrong (incorrect)
die Familie (-n)	family
fangen	to catch
die Farbe (-n)	color, paint
fast	almost

faul	lazy, bad (fruit, vegetables)
Februar	February
die Fee (-n)	fairy
fegen	to sweep
der Fehler (-)	mistake
die Feier (-n)	party
das Feld (-er)	field (for crops)
das Fell (-e)	fur
der Fels (-en)	rock (stone)
das Fenster (-)	window
das Fernsehen	television, TV
der Fernseher (-)	television (set), TV (set)
fertig	ready
fertig machen	to finish
fertig sein	to have finished
fest/machen	to fix (attach)
fett	fat
das Feuer (-)	fire
das Feuerwehrauto (-s)	fire engine
die Feuerwehrfrau (-en)	firefighter (woman)
der Feuerwehrmann (Feuerwehrmänner)	firefighter (man)
finden	to find, to think (consider)
der Finger (-)	finger
der Fisch (-e)	fish
fit	fit (healthy)
flach	flat
die Flasche (-n)	bottle
der Fleck (-e or -en)	spot
die Fledermaus (Fledermäuse)	bat (animal)
das Fleisch	meat
flicken	to mend, to repair
die Fliege (-n)	fly (insect)
fliegen	to fly
das Flugzeug (-e)	plane
der Fluss (Flüsse)	river
das Fohlen (-)	foal
die Form (-en)	shape
das Foto (-s)	photo
das Fotoalbum (Fotoalben)	photo album
der Fotoapparat (-e)	camera
die Frage (-n)	question
fragen	to ask
die Frau (-en)	woman
frech	naughty, bad
frei	free (not restricted)
Freitag	Friday
fressen	to eat (of animals)
sich freuen	to be glad
der Freund (-e)	friend (boy)
die Freundin (-nen)	friend (girl)
freundlich	friendly
frieren	to freeze
frisch	fresh
der Frosch (Frösche)	frog

German word list

früh	early	der Gipfel (-)	peak (mountain)	helfen	to help
der Frühling	spring	die Giraffe (-n)	giraffe	hell	bright (light), light (color)
das Frühstück (-e)	breakfast	die Gitarre (-n)	guitar	der Helm (-e)	helmet
der Fuchs (Füchse)	fox	das Glas (Gläser)	glass, jar	das Hemd (-en)	shirt
fühlen	to feel (touch)	glatt	smooth, straight (hair)	die Henne (-n)	hen
sich fühlen	to feel (happy, sad)	eine Glatze haben	to be bald	heran/reichen	to reach
führen	to lead	glauben	to think	der Herbst	fall (season)
füllen	to fill	gleich	equal, same	herein	inside, in
der Füller (-)	pen (ink)	glücklich	happy	herunter	down
fünf	five	das Gold	gold	das Herz (-en)	heart
fünft-	fifth	golden	gold (golden)	heute	today
fünfzehn	fifteen	graben	to dig	heute Abend	this evening, tonight
fünfzig	fifty	die Grapefruit (-s)	grapefruit	heute Nacht	tonight (in the night)
funktionieren	to work (function)	das Gras	grass	die Hexe (-n)	witch
für	for	gratis	free (no cost)	hier	here
der Fuß (Füße)	foot, base	grau	gray	hierher	(to) here
der Fußball	soccer	der Griff (-e)	handle	die Himbeere (-n)	raspberry
füttern	to feed	groß	big, large, tall (person), great	der Himmel	sky
				hinauf/steigen	to climb
die Gabel (-n)	fork	die Größe (-n)	height, size	hinein	inside, in
gähnen	to yawn	die Großeltern	grandparents	hin/fallen	to fall over
die Gans (Gänse)	goose	die Großmutter		sich hin/knien	to kneel (down)
ganz	quite (completely)	(Großmütter)	grandmother	sich hin/legen	to lie (down)
der Garten		die Großstadt		sich hin/setzen	to sit (down)
(Gärten)	garden	(Großstädte)	city	hinten	at the back
das Gas (-e)	gas	der Großvater		hinter	behind, at the back of
der Gast (Gäste)	guest, visitor	(Großväter)	grandfather	hinunter	down
das Gebäude (-)	building	grün	green	hinzu/fügen	to add (things)
geben	to give	die Gruppe (-n)	group	der Hirsch (-e)	deer
der Geburtstag		die Gurke (-n)	cucumber	hoch	high, tall (building)
(-e)	birthday	der Gürtel (-)	belt	hoch/heben	to lift
das Gedicht (-e)	poem	gut	good, well	der Hochstuhl	
gefährlich	dangerous			(Hochstühle)	highchair
gefrieren	to freeze	die Haarbürste (-n)	hairbrush	der Hocker (-)	stool
der Gefrierschrank		die Haare	hair	hoh-	high, tall (building)
(Gefrierschränke)	freezer	haben	to have	die Höhe (-n)	height (house, mountain)
gegen . . . fahren	to crash into	das Hähnchen (-)	chicken (cooked)		
der Gegensatz		der Hai (-e)	shark	die Höhle (-n)	cave
(Gegensätze)	opposite	halb	half	das Holz	wood
gegenüber	opposite (facing)	der Halbmond (-e)	crescent	das Holzscheit (-e)	log (for fire)
gegenüber/stehen	to face	die Hälfte (-n)	half (portion)	der Honig	honey
das Geheimnis		hallo	hello	hören	to hear
(-se)	secret	der Hals (Hälse)	neck	der Hotdog (-s)	hotdog
gehen	to go (on foot)	die Halskette (-n)	necklace	das Hotel (-s)	hotel
gehören	to belong	halten	to hold	hübsch	pretty
gelb	yellow	der Hamburger (-)	burger, hamburger	der Hubschrauber	
das Geld	money	der Hammer		(-)	helicopter
das Gemüse	vegetables	(Hämmer)	hammer	der Hügel (-)	hill
geöffnet	open	der Hamster (-)	hamster	das Huhn	
gerade	straight (line), even (number), upright (person)	die Hand (Hände)	hand	(Hühner)	hen
		der Handschuh (-e)	glove	der Hund (-e)	dog
		das Handtuch		das Hündchen (-)	puppy
das Geräusch (-e)	noise, sound	(Handtücher)	towel	hundert	hundred
gern	with pleasure, gladly	hängen	to hang	Hunger haben	to be hungry
geröntgt werden	to have an x-ray	hart	hard (surface)	hüpfen	to hop
das Geschenk (-e)	present, gift	hassen	to hate	der Hut (Hüte)	hat
die Geschichte (-n)	story	hässlich	ugly		
das Gesicht (-er)	face	der, die, das		die Idee (-n)	idea
das Gespenst (-er)	ghost	Haupt-	main	immer	always
gestern	yesterday	das Haus (Häuser)	house	in	inside, in, into
das Getränk (-e)	drink	der Hausschuh (-e)	slipper	das Insekt (-en)	insect
die		das Haustier (-e)	pet	die Insel (-n)	island
Getreideflocken	cereal	die Haut	skin	das Internet	Internet, Net, World Wide Web
gewinnen	to win	heiß	hot		
gewöhnlich	usually, usual	heizen	to heat (a room)		

irgendwo	somewhere, anywhere
ja	yes
die Jacke (-n)	jacket
jagen	to chase, to hunt
das Jahr (-e)	year
die Jahreszeit (-en)	season
Januar	January
die Jeans	jeans
jeder, jede, jedes	each, every
jemand	somebody, someone, anybody, anyone
jetzt	now
der Job (-s)	job
jonglieren	to juggle
jucken	to itch
Juli	July
jung	young
der Junge (-n)	boy
Juni	June
der Käfer (-)	beetle, bug
der Kaffee	coffee
der Käfig (-e)	cage
das Kalb (Kälber)	calf
kalt	cold
das Kamel (-e)	camel
der Kamm (Kämme)	comb
kämpfen	to fight
das Känguru (-s)	kangaroo
das Kaninchen (-)	rabbit
die Kante (-n)	edge
kaputt/machen	to break (machine)
die Karotte (-n)	carrot
die Karte (-n)	card, map, ticket
die Kartoffel (-n)	potato
der Karton (-s)	box (cardboard)
der Käse	cheese
das Kätzchen (-)	kitten
die Katze (-n)	cat
kaufen	to buy
kehren	to sweep
kein, keine, kein, keine	no (not any)
der Kellner (-)	waiter
die Kellnerin (-nen)	waitress
kennen	to know (people)
die Kerze (-n)	candle
kicken	to kick
der Kieselstein (-e)	pebble
das Kind (-er)	child
das Kinn (-e)	chin
die Kirsche (-n)	cherry
die Kiste (-n)	box (big)
die Klasse (-n)	class
das Klassenzimmer (-)	classroom
das Klavier (-e)	piano
kleben	to stick
der Klebstoff (-e)	glue
das Kleid (-er)	dress
die Kleider	clothes
klein	small, young (children)

kleiner werden	to shrink
das Kleinkind (-er)	toddler
klingeln	to ring
die Klinke (-n)	handle (door)
klopfen	to knock (on a door)
knall-	bright (color)
das Knie (-)	knee
knien	to kneel (be kneeling)
der Knöchel (-)	ankle
der Knochen (-)	bone
der Knopf (Knöpfe)	button
der Knoten (-)	knot
der Koch (Köche)	chef (man)
kochen	to cook
die Köchin (-nen)	chef (woman)
der Koffer (-)	suitcase
komisch	funny (strange)
kommen	to come
der König (-e)	king
die Königin (-nen)	queen
der Kopf (Köpfe)	head
das Kopfkissen (-)	pillow
der Kopfsalat (-e)	lettuce
der Korb (Körbe)	basket
der Körper (-)	body
kostenlos	free (no cost)
krabbeln	to crawl (baby)
kräftig	strong
das Krankenhaus (Krankenhäuser)	hospital
die Krankenschwester (-n)	nurse
der Krankenwagen (-)	ambulance
die Kreide	chalk
der Kreis (-e)	circle
das Kreuz (-e)	cross, x
kriechen	to crawl
das Krokodil (-e)	crocodile
die Krone (-n)	crown
die Küche (-n)	kitchen
der Kuchen (-)	cake
der Kugelschreiber (-)	pen (ballpoint)
die Kuh (Kühe)	cow
der Kühlschrank (Kühlschränke)	refrigerator
das Küken (-)	chick
der Kuli (-s)	pen (ballpoint)
die Kunst	art
der Künstler (-)	artist (man)
die Künstlerin (-nen)	artist (woman)
der Kürbis (-se)	pumpkin
kurz	short
die kurze Hose	shorts
der Kuss (Küsse)	kiss
küssen	to kiss
lächeln	to smile
lachen	to laugh
der Lack	paint (on metal)

das Lamm (Lämmer)	lamb
die Lampe (-n)	lamp
das Land (Länder)	country, land
die Landkarte (-n)	map
lang	long
die Länge (-n)	length
langsam	slow, slowly
langweilig	dull (boring)
der Lärm	noise (loud)
lassen	to let
der Lastwagen (-)	truck
das Lätzchen (-)	bib
laufen	to walk, to run, to rush (move quickly)
laut	loud, noisy
läuten	to ring
leben	to live (be alive)
das Leben (-)	life
die Lebensmittel	food (groceries)
lecken	to lick
lecker	delicious
leer	empty
legen	to put
der Lehrer (-)	teacher (man)
die Lehrerin (-nen)	teacher (woman)
leicht	easy, light (not heavy)
leise	quiet
die Leiter (-n)	ladder
lernen	to learn, to study
lesen	to read
letzt-	last
die Leute	people
das Licht (-er)	light
lieb (lieber, liebe)	dear, kind, friendly
lieben	to love
das Lied (-er)	song
liegen	to lie (be lying down)
liegen lassen	to leave (something)
das Lineal (-e)	ruler
die Linie (-n)	line (on paper)
link-	left (not right)
links	left (not right)
die Lippe (-n)	lip
die Liste (-n)	list
das Loch (Löcher)	hole
der Löffel (-)	spoon
los sein	to happen
der Löwe (-n)	lion
die Luft	air
der Luftballon (-s)	balloon
lügen	to lie (tell a lie)
lustig	funny (amusing)
machen	to do, to make
das Mädchen (-)	girl
die Mahlzeit (-en)	meal
Mai	May
malen	to paint (a picture)
manchmal	sometimes
der Mann (Männer)	man

German word list

die Mannschaft (-en) team
der Mantel (Mäntel) coat
der Marienkäfer (-) ladybug
die Marionette (-n) puppet (on strings)
der Markt (Märkte) market
März March
die Maschine (-n) machine
das Match (-e) match (game)
der Matrose (-n) sailor (man)
die Matrosin (-nen) sailor (woman)
matt dull (color)
die Mauer (-n) wall (outside)
die Maus (Mäuse) mouse
das Medikament (-e) medicine
das Meer (-e) sea
das Meer- schweinchen (-) guinea pig
das Mehl flour
mehr more
meinen to think
meist- most
die Menge (-n) amount
der Mensch (-en) person
messen to measure
das Messer (-) knife
das Metall (-e) metal
der Metzger (-) butcher
die Mikrowelle (-n) microwave
die Milch milk
die Minute (-n) minute
mischen to mix
mit with, by (car, bus)
Mitglied werden to join (a club)
mit/nehmen to take
das Mittagessen (-) lunch
die Mitte middle
das Mittel (-) medicine
mitten in the middle, in the center
Mittwoch Wednesday
das Modell (-e) model
mögen to like
der Monat (-e) month
der Mond (-e) moon
Montag Monday
morgen tomorrow
der Morgen (-) morning
das Motorrad (Motorräder) motorcycle
der Motorroller (-) scooter (with motor)
der Mund (Münder) mouth
die Münze (-n) coin
die Muschel (-n) shell (sea)
die Musik music
müssen to need to, to have to
die Mutter (Mütter) mother
Mutti Mom
die Mütze (-n) cap

nach after, to (a town or country)
nach/ahmen to copy (actions)
der Nachbar (-n) neighbor (man)
die Nachbarin (-nen) neighbor (woman)
der Nachmittag (-e) afternoon
nachmittags in the afternoon
die Nachricht (-en) news, message
nächst- next
die Nacht (Nächte) night
der Nachtfalter (-) moth
nackt bare
die Nacktschnecke (-n) slug
die Nadel (-n) needle
der Nagel (Nägel) nail
nahe close
in der Nähe (von) close (to)
nähen to sew
der Name (-n) name
die Nase (-n) nose
das Nashorn (Nashörner) rhinoceros, rhino
nass wet
die Natur nature
neben beside, next to, by
nehmen to take
sich neigen to lean (to one side)
nein no
nennen to call (name)
das Nest (-er) nest
nett nice, kind, friendly
das Netz (-e) net, web (spider's)
neu new
das Neueste news
neun nine
neunt- ninth
neunzehn nineteen
neunzig ninety
nicht not
nicht leiden können to hate
nichts nothing
nicht tief shallow, not deep
nicken to nod
nie never
niedlich cute, sweet
niedrig low
niemand no one
das Nilpferd (-e) hippopotamus, hippo
nirgends nowhere
noch still, yet
noch ein, eine, ein another
noch einmal again, once more
normalerweise usually
die Note (-n) note (music)
die Notiz (-en) note (message)
das Notizbuch (Notizbücher) notebook
November November
null zero
die Nummer (-n) number (street, phone)
nur only

die Nuss (Nüsse) nut
nützlich useful

oben on top
das Obst fruit
oder or
offen open
öffnen to open
oft often
ohne without
das Ohr (-en) ear
Oktober October
das Öl oil
Oma Granny
der Onkel (-) uncle
Opa Grandpa
die Orange (-n) orange (fruit)
orangefarben orange (color)
der Ort (-e) place
das Oval (-e) oval
der Ozean (-e) ocean

das Paar (-e) pair
ein paar some
der Palast (Paläste) palace
der Papagei (-en) parrot
das Papier (-e) paper
die Paprikaschote (-n) pepper (vegetable)
der Park (-s or -e) park
parken to park
die Party (-s) party
passen to fit
passieren to happen
der Pelz (-e) fur
die Person (-en) person
der Pfad (-e) path
der Pfeffer pepper (spice)
das Pferd (-e) horse
der Pfirsich (-e) peach
die Pflanze (-n) plant
die Pflaume (-n) plum
pflücken to pick (flowers, fruit)
die Pfote (-n) paw
die Pfütze (-n) puddle
das Picknick (-e or -s) picnic
der Pilot (-en) pilot (man)
die Pilotin (-nen) pilot (woman)
der Pilz (-e) mushroom
der Pinguin (-e) penguin
die Pizza (Pizzas or Pizzen) pizza
der Plan (Pläne) plan
planen to plan
der Planet (-en) planet
der Platz (Plätze) place, space, room, seat
plötzlich suddenly
der Po (-s) bottom
die Polizei police
das Polizeiauto (-s) police car
das Pony (-s) pony
der Preis (-e) price, prize
der Prinz (-en) prince

die Prinzessin (-nen)	princess
probieren	to try, to taste (take a little)
der Punkt (-e)	point (score), spot
die Puppe (-n)	doll, puppet
putzen	to clean
das Puzzle (-s)	jigsaw puzzle
das Quadrat (-e)	square
quaken	to quack
das Quiz (-)	quiz
das Rad (Räder)	wheel, bicycle
mit dem Rad fahren	to cycle, to ride a bike
das Radio (-s)	radio
die Rakete (-n)	rocket
der Rand (Ränder)	edge
raten	to guess
das Rätsel (-)	puzzle (wordgame)
die Ratte (-n)	rat
das Raumfahrzeug (-e)	spacecraft
die Raupe (-n)	caterpillar
die Rechen- aufgabe (-n)	sum (math), math problem
recht-	right (not left)
das Rechteck (-e)	rectangle
rechts	right (not left)
das Regal (-e)	shelf
der Regen	rain
der Regenbogen (-)	rainbow
der Regenschirm (-e)	umbrella
regnen	to rain
reich	rich
reichen	to pass (give)
reif	ripe
die Reihe (-n)	line (of people)
der Reis	rice
die Reise (-n)	journey
der Reißverschluss (Reißverschlüsse)	zipper
reiten	to ride (a horse)
rennen	to run
reparieren	to fix, to mend, to repair
retten	to save (from danger), to rescue
richtig	right, true
richtig schreiben können	to spell
riechen	to smell
der Riese (-n)	giant
riesig	enormous
die Rinde (-n)	bark (of tree)
der Ring (-e)	ring
der Ritter (-)	knight
der Roboter (-)	robot
der Rock (Röcke)	skirt
die Rockmusik	rock (music)

der Roller (-)	scooter
Rollschuh laufen	to skate (on rollerskates)
das Röntgenbild (-er)	x-ray
rosa	pink
die Rose (-n)	rose
die Rosine (-n)	raisin
rot	red
die Rote Bete	beetroot
der Rücken (-)	back
rufen	to call, to shout
ruhig	quiet, calm
rund	round
die Rutschbahn (-en)	slide
rutschen	to slide
die Sache (-n)	thing
der Saft (Säfte)	juice
die Säge (-n)	saw
sagen	to say, to tell
die Salami	salami
der Salat (-e)	salad
das Salz	salt
Samstag	Saturday
der Sand	sand
die Sandale (-n)	sandal
sanft	gentle
satt	full (after eating)
der Sattel (Sättel)	saddle
der Satz (Sätze)	sentence
sauber	clean
die Schachtel (-n)	box (small)
das Schaf (-e)	sheep
der Schal (-s or -e)	scarf
die Schale (-n)	skin (fruit, vegetable), shell (eggs, nuts)
scharf	sharp (edge)
der Schatten (-)	shadow
der Schauer (-)	shower (of rain)
die Schaukel (-n)	swing
schaukeln	to swing
der Schauspieler (-)	actor
die Schauspielerin (-nen)	actress
die Scheibe (-n)	slice
schenken	to give (as a gift)
die Schere (-n)	scissors
die Scheune (-n)	barn
schicken	to send
schieben	to push
das Schiff (-e)	ship
das Schild (-er)	sign (on road)
der Schild (-e)	peak (on cap)
der Schirm (-e)	peak (on cap)
schlafen	to sleep, to be asleep
das Schlafzimmer (-)	bedroom
schlagen	to hit
sich schlagen mit	to fight
der Schläger (-)	bat (for sports)
der Schlamm	mud
die Schlange (-n)	snake
schlecht	bad

schleichen	to creep
schließen	to close, to shut
Schlittschuh laufen	to skate (on ice)
das Schloss (Schlösser)	castle, palace, lock
der Schlüssel (-)	key
schmecken	to taste
der Schmetterling (-e)	butterfly
schmutzig	dirty
der Schnabel (Schnäbel)	beak
die Schnecke (-n)	snail
der Schnee	snow
schneiden	to cut
schneien	to snow
schnell	quick, fast
der Schnupfen (-)	cold
die Schokolade	chocolate
schön	beautiful, nice
schreiben	to write
der Schreibtisch (-e)	desk
schreien	to shout (very loudly)
der Schuh (-e)	shoe
die Schule (-n)	school
der Schüler (-)	pupil (boy)
die Schülerin (-nen)	pupil (girl)
der Schulhof (Schulhöfe)	playground (school)
die Schulter (-n)	shoulder
die Schüssel (-n)	bowl
schütteln	to shake
der Schwamm (Schwämme)	sponge
der Schwan (Schwäne)	swan
der Schwanz (Schwänze)	tail
schwarz	black
schweben	to float (in air)
schwer	heavy, difficult, hard
die Schwester (-n)	sister
schwierig	difficult, hard
das Schwimmbad (Schwimmbäder)	(swimming) pool
das Schwimm- becken (-)	(swimming) pool
schwimmen	to swim, to float
sechs	six
sechst-	sixth
sechzehn	sixteen
sechzig	sixty
der See (-n)	lake
die See	sea
der Seehund (-e)	seal
sehen	to see
sehr	very
sehr gern mögen	to love
seicht	shallow
die Seife	soap
das Seil (-e)	rope
seit	since (time)
die Seite (-n)	side, page
seltsam	odd (strange)

German word list

senkrecht	upright (wall, pillar)
September	September
setzen	to put
das Shampoo	shampoo
die Shorts	shorts
sicher	safe, sure
sieben	seven
siebt-	seventh
siebzehn	seventeen
siebzig	seventy
singen	to sing
sinken	to sink
der Sitz (-e)	seat (chair)
sitzen	to sit (be sitting)
Ski fahren	to ski
so	so (so big)
die Socke (-n)	sock
das Sofa (-s)	sofa
der Sohn (Söhne)	son
der Soldat (-en)	soldier
der Sommer	summer
die Sonne	sun
die Sonnenblume (-n)	sunflower
die Sonnenbrille (-n)	sunglasses
Sonntag	Sunday
die Sorte (-n)	kind, sort
sparen	to save (time, money)
der Spaß	fun
spät	late
der Spiegel (-)	mirror
ein Spiegelei machen	to fry an egg
das Spiel (-e)	game, match
spielen	to play
der Spielplatz (Spielplätze)	playground (in park)
die Spielsachen	toys
das Spielzeug (-e)	toy
der Spinat	spinach
die Spinne (-n)	spider
spitz	sharp (point)
die Spitze (-n)	tip, point
der Sport (-e)	sport
die Sprache (-n)	language
sprechen	to speak, to talk
springen	to jump, to dive
spritzen	to splash
das Spülbecken (-)	sink (kitchen)
stabil	strong (solid)
die Stadt (Städte)	town, city
die Stange (-n)	bar
der Star (-s)	star (person)
stark	strong
statt	instead of
der Staubsauger (-)	vacuum cleaner
stechen	to sting
stecken	to put (inside)
stehen	to stand
steil	steep
der Stein (-e)	stone, rock
die Stelle (-n)	place, job
stellen	to put

sterben	to die
der Stern (-e)	star (in sky)
der Stiefel (-)	boot
der Stiel (-e)	handle (of pan)
still	quiet, still
die Stimme (-n)	voice
der Stock (Stöcke)	stick
stoßen	to bump
der Strand (Strände)	beach
die Straße (-n)	street, road
streichen	to paint (a room)
das Streichholz (Streichhölzer)	match (for fire)
der Strom	electricity
das Stück (-e)	piece, slice (of cake)
der Stuhl (Stühle)	chair
die Stunde (-n)	hour, lesson
der Sturm (Stürme)	storm
sich stützen	to lean (on)
suchen	to search
die Summe (-n)	sum, math problem
der Supermarkt (Supermärkte)	supermarket
die Suppe (-n)	soup
süß	sweet
der Tag (-e)	day
die Tante (-n)	aunt
tanzen	to dance
tapfer	brave
die Tasche (-n)	bag, pocket
die Tasse (-n)	cup
die Tatsache (-n)	fact
tauchen	to dive (underwater)
der Taucher (-)	diver
tausend	thousand
das Taxi (-s)	taxi
der Teddy (-s)	teddy bear
der Tee	tea
der Teich (-e)	pond
das Teil (-e)	part, piece
teilen	to share
das Telefon (-e)	telephone, phone
der Teller (-)	plate
der Teppich (-e)	carpet, rug (big)
der Teppichboden (Teppichböden)	carpet
teuer	expensive
tief	deep
die Tiefkühltruhe (-n)	freezer
das Tier (-e)	animal
der Tiergarten (Tiergärten)	zoo
der Tiger (-)	tiger
der Tintenfisch (-e)	octopus
der Tisch (-e)	table
der Toast	toast
die Tochter (Töchter)	daughter
die Toilette (-n)	toilet
toll	great (fantastic)
die Tomate (-n)	tomato

der Ton (Töne)	sound
das Tor (-e)	gate, goal
töten	to kill
tragen	to carry, to wear
der Traktor (-en)	tractor
die Traube (-n)	grape
der Traum (Träume)	dream
träumen	to dream
traurig	sad
sich treffen	to meet (by arrangement)
die Treppe	stairs
trinken	to drink
trocken	dry
trocknen	to dry
die Trommel (-n)	drum
der Tropfen (-)	drop (of liquid)
der Truthahn (Truthähne)	turkey
das T-Shirt (-s)	T-shirt
tun	to do
tun als ob	to pretend
die Tür (-en)	door
die Tüte (-n)	bag (plastic, paper)
über	over, across, about (story)
überall	everywhere
überqueren	to cross
die Überraschung (-en)	surprise
die Überschwemmung (-en)	flood
Uhr	o'clock, time (what time is it?)
die Uhr (-en)	clock, watch
um	around, at (a time)
umarmen	to hug
der Umschlag (Umschläge)	envelope
umsonst	free (no cost)
um/stellen	to move (an object)
um/stoßen	to knock (over)
um . . . zu	to (in order to)
unartig	naughty
und	and
einen Unfall haben	to crash, to have an accident
ungefähr	about (roughly)
ungerade	uneven (number)
unglücklich	unhappy
unrecht	wrong (bad)
unten	at the bottom
unter	under, below
unter/gehen	to sink
sich unterhalten	to talk
unterschreiben	to sign
die Untertasse (-n)	saucer
die Vase (-n)	vase
der Vater (Väter)	father
Vati	Dad
sich verabschieden	to say goodbye
verbinden	to join

verbrennen	to burn
verbringen	to spend (time)
die Vergangenheit	past
vergessen	to forget
verkaufen	to sell
verkehrt herum	upside down
verlassen	to leave (a place or a person)
verlieren	to lose
vermissen	to miss (someone)
verpassen	to miss (bus, train)
verrühren	to stir, to mix
verschieden	different
verschütten	to spill
verschwinden	to disappear
versprechen	to promise
verspritzen	to splash
verstecken	to hide (something)
sich verstecken	to hide (yourself)
verstehen	to understand
versuchen	to try
viel	much, a lot
viele	many, a lot, lots
vielleicht	maybe
vier	four
viert-	fourth
das Viertel (-)	quarter
vierzehn	fourteen
vierzig	forty
violett	purple
der Vogel (Vögel)	bird
voll	full
von	from, by (done by)
vor	before, in front of
voran/gehen	to lead (go ahead)
vorbei/gehen	to pass (go past)
der, die, das Vorder-	front
die Vorderseite (-n)	front
der Vorleger (-)	rug (small)
der Vormittag (-e)	morning
wachsen	to grow (get bigger)
der Wachsmalstift (-e)	crayon
der Wagen (-)	car
wählen	to choose
wahr	true
während	while
der Wal (-e)	whale
der Wald (Wälder)	woods, forest
die Wand (Wände)	wall (inside)
wann?	when? (in questions)
warm	warm
warten	to wait
warum	why
was	what
das Waschbecken (-)	sink (bathroom)
waschen	to wash (something)
sich waschen	to wash (yourself)
die Wasch- maschine (-n)	washing machine

das Wasser	water
wecken	to wake (someone)
der Wecker (-)	alarm clock
der Weg (-e)	path, way (route)
weg/nehmen	to take (away)
weh/tun	to hurt
weich	soft, smooth (skin)
die Weide (-n)	field (for animals)
Weihnachten	Xmas
weil	because
weinen	to cry
weiß	white
weit	wide, far
welcher?, welche?, welches?, welche?	which? (in questions)
die Welle (-n)	wave
die Welt	world
der Weltraum	space (outer space)
wenige	few
weniger	less
wenn	if, when
wer?	who? (in questions)
werfen	to throw
das Wetter	weather
das Wettrennen (-)	race
wichtig sein	to matter, to be important
wie	like, how, what . . . like?
wie alt	how old
wieder	again
wie viel	how much
wie viele	how many
wild	wild
der Wind (-e)	wind
winken	to wave
der Winter	winter
winzig	tiny
wirklich	real (not imaginary)
wissen	to know (facts)
der Witz (-e)	joke
wo	where
die Woche (-n)	week
wohnen	to live (somewhere), to stay (visit)
die Wolke (-n)	cloud
wollen	to want
das Wort (Wörter or Worte)	word
das Wörterbuch (Wörterbücher)	dictionary
der Wunsch (Wünsche)	wish
sich etwas wünschen	to make a wish
die Wurst (Würste)	sausage
die Wüste (-n)	desert
die Wüstenspring- maus (Wüsten- springmäuse)	gerbil
das Xylophon (-e)	xylophone
die Zahl (-en)	number (figure)
zahlen	to pay

der Zahn (Zähne)	tooth
der Zahnarzt (Zahnärzte)	dentist (man)
die Zahnärztin (-nen)	dentist (woman)
die Zahnbürste (-n)	toothbrush
die Zahnpasta	toothpaste
zart	pale (color), soft
der, die, das Zauber-	magic
die Zauberkunst	magic
der Zauberspruch (Zaubersprüche)	spell (magic)
der Zaun (Zäune)	fence
das Zebra (-s)	zebra
die Zehe (-n)	toe
zehn	ten
zehnt-	tenth
das Zeichen (-)	sign (symbol)
zeichnen	to draw
die Zeichnung (-en)	drawing
zeigen	to show, to point
die Zeit	time
die Zeitung (-en)	newspaper
das Zelt (-e)	tent
zelten	to camp
zerbrechen	to break
das Zicklein (-)	kid (baby goat)
die Ziege (-n)	goat
ziehen	to pull, to grow (cultivate)
ziemlich	quite (fairly)
das Zimmer (-)	room (in house)
die Zitrone (-n)	lemon
der Zoo (-s)	zoo
zu	to (a place), too (hot or cold)
der Zucker	sugar
zu Ende	over (finished)
zuerst	first
zu Fuß gehen	to walk, to go on foot
der Zug (Züge)	train
zu Hause	at home
zuletzt	last
zu/machen	to close, to shut
die Zunge (-n)	tongue
zusammen	together
zusammen/falten	to fold
zusammen/passen	to match
zusammen/zählen	to add (numbers)
zu/werfen	to throw (to someone)
zu/winken	to wave (to someone)
zwanzig	twenty
zwei	two
der Zweig (-e)	branch, stick
zweit-	second
die Zwiebel (-n)	onion
der Zwilling (-e)	twin
zwischen	between
zwölf	twelve

Hear the words on the Internet

If you can use the Internet and your computer can play sounds, you can listen to all the German words and phrases in this dictionary, read by a German person.

Go to the Usborne Quicklinks Website at **www.usborne-quicklinks.com** Type in the keywords **german picture dictionary** and follow the simple instructions. Try listening to the words or phrases and then saying them yourself. This will help you learn to speak German easily and well.

Always follow the safety rules on the right when you are using the Internet.

What you need

To play the German words, your computer may need a small program called an audio player, such as

RealPlayer® or Windows® Media Player. These programs are free, and if you don't already have one, you can download a copy from **www.usborne-quicklinks.com**

Internet safety rules

- Ask your parent's, guardian's or teacher's permission before you connect to the Internet.
- When you are on the Internet, never tell anyone your full name, address or telephone number, and ask an adult before you give your email address.
- If a website asks you to log in or register by typing your name or email address, ask an adult's permission first.
- If you receive an email from someone you don't know, tell an adult and do not reply to the email.

Notes for parents or guardians

The Picture Dictionary area of the Usborne Quicklinks Website contains no links to external websites. However, other areas of Usborne Quicklinks do contain links to websites that do not belong to Usborne Publishing. The links are regularly reviewed and updated, but Usborne Publishing is not responsible, and does not accept liability, for the content or availability of any website other than its own, or for any exposure to harmful,

offensive or inaccurate material which may appear on the Web.

We recommend that children are supervised while on the Internet, that they do not use Internet chat rooms and that you use Internet filtering software to block unsuitable material. Please ensure that your children follow the safety guidelines above. For more information, see the "Net Help" area on the Usborne Quicklinks Website at **www.usborne-quicklinks.com**

RealPlayer® is a trademark of RealNetworks, Inc., registered in the US and other countries. Windows® is a trademark of Microsoft Corporation, registered in the US and other countries.

With thanks to Staedtler for providing the Fimo® material for models. Bruder® toys supplied by Euro Toys and Models Ltd. Additional models by Les Pickstock, Barry Jones, Stef Lumley, Karen Krige and Stefan Barnett Americanization editor: Carrie Armstrong

First published in 2004 by Usborne Publishing Ltd, 83-85 Saffron Hill, London EC1N 8RT, England. www.usborne.com